CURVY ALL THE WAY

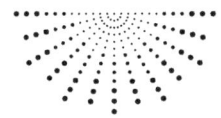

KELSIE STELTING

For anyone who's struggled finding the right size in the store - clothes should be made to fit you, not the other way around.

CONTENTS

BETHANY

*A*s I rounded the corner of Main and North, the Garland Christmas tree came into sight, a giant evergreen cone standing out in Cider Center. In the dusky sky, I could just make out the garland going around the branches and the brightly colored baubles. But soon it would be all lit up. Soon, I could make my wish.

I pulled my hat down over my ears, continuing toward the tree. My nose felt like an icicle and my fingertips were numb.

I always did get cold easily, but even so, I loved Garland during the Christmas season. There was nothing like it in the world, which meant people came from all over to celebrate. No other place did Christmas like this town.

I walked a little faster, sure that the rest of my friends had beaten me there.

As I worked my way through dozens and dozens of people, I spotted my four best friends, Belle, Carol, Holly, and Sera, near the front of the crowd. They were my favorite people in the whole world, and I wholeheartedly believed they were a part of what made Garland special. We had been friends for years.

Every year, on this day, Belle made sure to find a good spot at the very front so we could have the best view of the Christmas tree lighting. This year was no different. If she could've set up a tent the night before and gotten a better spot, I was sure she would.

I gave them each a hug and we settled in, excitement permeating the air around us with the growing crowd's chatter.

"I can't wait," Belle said with glee. She wholeheartedly believed in the town legend that if you wished upon the star just as the mayor lit it up, then your wish would come true.

I knew better. Forcing a smile, I said, "I can't wait for some hot chocolate after this."

"Not a bad idea," Sera chimed in, shivering a little.

I stared up at the tree, hands shoved in my coat pockets for extra warmth. My friends looked so hopeful, even Carol, who struggled with the Christmas season since her parents' divorce. But I couldn't help the pang of sadness that hit at the thought of making yet another wish that didn't come true.

Every year up until now, I'd made the same wish: that my brother's best friend would finally notice me as more than his best friend's dorky little sister.

I still remembered the first time my brother, Eli, brought Kane over to our house. They were ten and I was nine. While they practiced baseball in the back yard, I helped mom with the dishes. She kept wincing every time they threw the ball off course, worried they'd lose it over the fence or bust a window. But me? I couldn't take my eyes off Kane. He was so cute, with dark brown skin, short black hair, and so much confidence in his every move. Unlike me, who'd just gone through a growth spurt and was still knocking over glasses at every meal.

But after years of wishing for him to notice me with no results, I was beginning to think it was impossible for him to return my crush. As much as the disappointment hurt, I knew it was time to let the wish go.

As the mayor rose up with the help of a firefighter truck ladder, I considered my wish. A different wish.

The mayor gently placed the star on top of the tree, said a few words about the holiday season, and just a second later, the star shone brightly from its perch.

In that instant, I closed my eyes and wished for a chance at my one big dream. Hopefully this wish *did* have a chance of coming true.

I wish to get into the fashion program of my dreams. I thought the words with all my heart, willing it to come true.

The application deadline for the Future Fashion Icon Summer Program was January first, and it was going to be super competitive to snag a spot, but I was applying anyway. Plus-size clothing designers didn't usually make it, but I was desperate to make cute clothing available to girls and women just like me. We deserved to feel beautiful, too, not stuck wearing loud, ugly prints and cold-shoulder shirts.

Please, please let me earn a spot, I wished again for extra measure.

Then I exhaled and opened my eyes. Everyone around me was clapping and cheering. Parents pointed and smiled in awe and kids jumped up and down.

I joined in the clapping, feeling a little emotional all of a sudden. I wasn't sure what I'd do if yet another wish didn't come true.

Belle's eyes met mine, and she gave me a look that asked, *Are you okay?*

Embarrassed, I wiped a tear from the corner of my eye and nodded. Even so, she put her arm around my shoulder. I felt better already, knowing I'd have my friends no matter what.

As the crowd started to disperse, my friends and I gathered around in a circle, wondering out loud about the other big Garland tradition.

Every year for the last century, someone got the job of being Santa Claus. It was a big deal to get the honor, and most of all, no one could ever know Santa's true identity.

"Maybe it'll be Mr. Thornton," Carolyn joked.

We all collectively shuddered at the thought of our old, nose-picking math teacher dawning the Santa suit.

As we began walking away from Cider Center,

we kept making guesses at the next Santa Claus, each one more and more ludicrous.

"I'm going to miss you guys," I told them as we reached Cocoa Corner, the coffee shop in town.

The five of us were going to be pretty busy for the next couple of weeks. My brother and parents were traveling before Christmas for him to visit a college, and I was staying with my grandma to focus on my application. I still needed one big, showstopping piece to add. Everyone else had something going on as well, so we agreed to meet back up at Haley's big New Year's Eve party and catch up again.

"New Year's will be here before we know it," Belle said. "And I bet we'll all have something fun and interesting to share." There was a twinkle in her eye I couldn't quite explain.

I saw Carolynn roll her eyes a bit, but I put my arm around her. "I bet we will."

After that, we were off.

I had a big mug of hot chocolate on my mind. Sipping it in the coffee shop while putting the finishing touches on my plan sounded like the perfect end to the night before going back home to say goodbye to my parents and brother.

I had no idea if that wish I made would do me any good, but I did know that I needed all the help I could get, including a little bit of Garland magic.

2
KANE

I could remember the day I sold my first snowball.

I was twelve years old, having a snowball fight with some of my friends near Cider Center. It was going to be the most epic snowball fight of all time, and I was determined to win.

So, I showed up earlier than anyone else, packing snowballs and building them into a pile so my team would have an unlimited supply, leading us to a certain victory without the hassle of constantly stooping to pack and build snowballs.

But something else happened that year.

Influenza A.

It contaminated the kids of Garland just as thoroughly as a fresh blanket of snow covered the ground. Only one other kid showed up to the snow battle, and I had way more snowballs than we needed.

Noticing that, a dad and his son asked if they could have some of my leftovers. When I said, "Okay," the dad gave me five dollars.

I walked away from the park staring at the crumpled bill. Abe stared back at me like we were both in on a secret.

It was the easiest money I'd ever made, and the possibilities with that much money were *endless*.

I could get a toy from the local store, Santa's Bag. I could pay one of my friends for a video game I wanted. I could even buy a few new baseballs without my parents' speeches about keeping track of my stuff and not hitting the balls hard enough to go over a fence.

And if one guy bought them from me—imagine how many other tourists would do the same.

I put that theory to the test, and over the years, the business had evolved.

Now I had a kiosk at Cider Center where people could buy snowballs or even pay me to sneak attack one of their friends. (That was a popular service.) I set up snowball fight dates for couples, prepped for photoshoots, and more.

Tonight was one of my busiest nights of the year; the lighting of the Garland Christmas tree always brought plenty of customers.

Even with hours of prep, I sold out. As I was flipping my sign from open to closed, my best friend, Eli, walked up. He didn't look as happy as usual, though we clapped hands and patted each other's back.

He gestured at my empty kiosk. "You cleaned up tonight."

I chuckled, rubbing the back of my neck. "Guess I did. Can't believe you're ditching me this year," I teased, trying to lighten the mood.

He and his parents were going to California for a week to check out a college that wanted him on their baseball team like Santa wanted cookies and milk. But since he had plenty of schools recruiting him, they wanted to make sure this one was the best fit for him.

Eli shook his head at me. "I don't feel bad for ditching you–just Bethany. I know she says she wants to stay home, but, I don't know... It's Christmastime."

Just at the mention of his little sister, my heart stood at attention.

Something happened a few years ago. Instead

of being my best friend's little sister, I started noticing little things about her…

Her brown eyes that turned amber when they caught the sunlight.

The way her red hair framed her heart-shaped face.

How her entire face lit up when she talked about fashion design…

But I had to keep all my feelings buried because everyone knew you couldn't date your best friend's little sister. It was bro code–and that stuff was sacred.

If Eli noticed all the thoughts going through my mind about his little sister, he definitely didn't show it. He continued on asking, "What are you doing now?"

I shrugged, bringing myself back to the present. "Not much to do in Garland that hasn't been done before."

"Movies?" he suggested.

I nodded. "Sure." We started walking toward the only movie theater in town, It's a Wonderful Film. Incidentally, all they played were Christmas movies. But the popcorn was the bomb.

Eli was quiet as we walked even though he usually never ran out of things to say.

"Nervous?" I asked. He was leaving with his parents tomorrow, bright and early.

He shook his head slightly. "Still thinking about Bethany."

Ironic, considering I needed to *stop* thinking about her. "She'll be fine–she's with your grandma," I reminded him.

We turned a corner, and now that we weren't on a main road, we were the only ones on the sidewalk.

"I know. It's just that..." He paused, and I could see he was feeling some sort of way about this. "I hate to leave her behind during Christmas. She says she has a big fashion project she's working on, so she *wants* to stay. But still, I kinda feel bad I'm the reason she'll be here while the rest of us are elsewhere."

"I get it," I replied. "I mean, despite all the ways you love to annoy her, I can tell you're a good big brother to her. And that is just so sweet."

That got him to sock me in the shoulder. I grinned, glad I'd been successful in lifting his mood a little bit. Eli wasn't one to always show it, but he had a good heart.

We reached the movie theater and headed

inside, getting our tickets along with a couple buckets of popcorn, extra butter on mine.

Luckily for us, the movie theater was doing a special showing of *Die Hard*, my personal favorite Christmas movie. Talk about Garland town controversy. There had been a whole five-page editorial about it in the newspaper when the movie was added to the movie theater's playlist when it was only supposed to play Christmas movies.

Who knew *Die Hard* was such a controversial topic?

We took our seats near the front, and I settled in, ready for a couple hours of primetime action.

But Eli still seemed overly worried about Bethany. I could tell. He hadn't dug into our popcorn yet. It was hard to relax when my friend was down. Considering the movie was about to start, I said, "Eli, what do we have to do for you to feel better about going? You know you can't stay home."

That's when his eyes lit up like there was a literal idea-lightbulb sparking. "You could watch out for her while I'm gone."

That caught me off guard. "Watch out for her?" I asked in a whisper.

A couple slid into the seats behind us, the lady quietly telling her husband that they better be seeing *The Polar Express* after this.

Eli gave them a glance before saying, "Yeah, man. Bethany. If you notice she seems lonely or something, you can spend time with her. She says she's fine, but you'll be there for her if she's not, right?"

For some reason, my best friend asking me to keep an eye on his sister made my stomach turn into a knot. But it's not like I could say no. He was my best friend, and he was worried about his little sister. "Yeah, man, I got you. Don't worry." I could worry enough for the both of us.

He finally seemed to exhale. "Thanks, man. I knew I could count on you."

After that, the lights dimmed, and Eli finally started eating his popcorn. He seemed to feel a thousand times better.

But I didn't.

What exactly had I committed to? And why did it make me nervous thinking of spending time together with Bethany?

She was my best friend's sister, and I'd always kept my distance.

Now my heart beat faster at the thought of

being alone with her, talking to her. Getting carried away with her.

No. That could *not* happen.

The movie started, but it was hard to stay focused on the plot.

I would keep my word to Eli, but I wouldn't go any further, I decided.

All I really needed to do was just keep an eye on her from afar. She would be fine, and I could tell Eli I fulfilled my promise.

That would be the best thing for everyone.

No need to get close to her.

3
BETHANY

*P*retty much everything I did in my life revolved around my dream of becoming a plus-size fashion icon. So, while most teenage girls would die at the thought of going to sewing club every Wednesday afternoon with their grandmother, I took it very seriously.

There were lots of talented ladies in the Garland sewing club, and I'd picked up some of my best tips and tricks from them. Plus, I always liked hearing them talk about how they grew up. Some of the things they'd done or witnessed growing up were really interesting. And some of it was just downright scandalous. (Have you ever had an eighty-year-old woman make you blush? Because I have!)

Handicrafts like sewing and knitting kept your hands busy, but best of all, it left you free to talk and listen.

"You call me if you need any help with that application of yours," Mrs. Cole told me on Wednesday as Grandma and I started packing up at the top of the hour.

Ms. Patty chimed in, "I really think you've got nothing to worry about, honey." She lay a heavily bejeweled hand on my shoulder for reassurance, and probably also to steady herself. She was getting up in age, but she could still pull off a mean rolled hem.

"Thank you both," I replied with a tentative smile. "I'm really nervous about the whole thing. I mean, there's a paper I have to write and designs I have to submit, but it also feels like the opportunity of a lifetime to show them what I've got." I exhaled, my chest a little tight. "I just hope it's the beginning of making a name for myself one day."

Grandma leaned over in her chair and put her arm around my shoulders. "If anyone's got the talent—"

"—and the dedication—" Mrs. Cole said, with her finger high in the air.

"—*and* the dedication," Grandma echoed, "it's you."

Grandma's brown eyes sparkled as she smiled at me, and that calmed my nerves down a little bit. It was nice knowing such talented seamstresses had so much faith in me.

But I also knew it was up to me to do my absolute best to earn my place in this fashion program.

It wasn't going to be easy, though.

As we left sewing club and headed back home, I couldn't help thinking about how much I had left to do, how many applications were going to be submitted to the program, and what my chances really were.

Especially because my focus was plus-size fashion. Everywhere I looked, people were saying plus-size fashion was a dead end, in both fashion and modeling. Most stores didn't even carry plus-size clothing–they offered it online only or not at all.

The lack of options made me so angry.

How could plus sizes and designs be so limited when there were so many plus-size girls and women who deserved to look and feel beautiful just as much as the girls who could fit a small, medium, or large?

I just didn't get it.

All of that was still swirling around in my mind as Grandma and I were passing the Cider Center, her cart rolling behind us. Grandma came to a stop, her eye on the snowball stand several feet away. "Look, it's that nice boy with the snowball business."

She began walking over to him, and I followed behind, my heart speeding up.

It was Kane. Kane was the one with the snowball business. Eli's extremely cute, very handsome best friend.

Did I mention he was very handsome?

Because he was.

And now Grandma and I were standing right in front of him.

His familiar grin greeted me. "Bethany. Mrs. Hart."

"Hello there, Kane," Grandma said kindly.

I gave him a small wave and smile.

Why was it so hard to act normally, much less remember to breathe, around him?

"How's the holiday season treating you and the business?" Grandma asked loudly.

One thing about Grandma. She loved stopping to chitchat with anyone and everyone in Garland.

Kane gave me a quick glance I couldn't quite

read before responding. "Pretty good, actually. One thing about Garland," he said with a chuckle, "everyone loves a good snowball fight."

Grandma laughed. "We sure do. And you know what, I think I'd like to purchase a snowball for old time's sake."

She began winding her arm around to stretch it, like she was getting ready for a pro softball game or something.

Kane handed her a pristine, large white snowball. I didn't have to hold it in my hands to know it was the perfect weight, the perfect consistency.

"Thank you," Grandma said. She passed him a dollar, took a few steps away, and quickly found a little boy who had some snowballs of his own but no one to play with.

Kane and I watched them play for a minute. We both chuckled when the kid got her back with a snowball.

"She's a hoot, isn't she?" Kane told me.

I laughed. "That's Grandma. Never a dull moment when you're with her."

When I turned to look at Kane and get his reaction, he looked like he was going to say something but then didn't.

Trying to fill the awkward silence, I said, "You

know, the town really loves your balls—I mean, snowballs."

OH MY GOD.

I wanted to melt into the snow itself and disappear forever.

My face quickly turned hot. Out of nowhere, little drops of sweat formed on my cheeks and my forehead, like I'd eaten the hottest pepper in the world.

Which actually would've been preferable to the comment I'd just made.

I didn't risk looking at Kane's face. Thankfully, Grandma came back over in that moment, and she thanked Kane before we went back on our way.

"He is such a nice boy," she told me, brushing snow off her coat.

"Uh huh," I managed, my face still really warm.

"He seems to like talking to you," she said, like she was telling me a juicy secret.

I tried to brush it off and held on tighter to my bag. "Oh, he's just nice. He's nice to everyone."

Besides, no matter how cute Kane was, it didn't matter if he only thought of me as his friend's kid sister.

He was my brother's best friend. He was

incredibly cute. A great guy. He could have any girl he wanted.

He would never want to be with a girl like me. That sort of thing didn't happen in the real world, not even here in the magical town of Garland.

The faster I could accept that, the easier it would be to focus on what really mattered: getting into the fashion program of my dreams.

4

KANE

*I*t wasn't long after Bethany and her grandmother left that a rambunctious family came by my snowball stand. "This is it!" the mom said to her kids. "The snowball shop!"

The town of Garland was pretty famous around the entire northeast for our year-round magical Christmas vibes, but I didn't realize my snowball stand was famous too.

"You've heard of it?" I asked them. The kids nodded eagerly, and she explained they'd been following my social media account for months and even saw Tiktoks posted by other tourists about my kiosk. "We are so excited to finally be here," she said with a grin.

She and her family all had matching hats and

sweaters. The oldest kid, a boy, looked like he was about nine. There was a girl who had to be maybe seven (a little younger than my little brother) and another boy who had to be four years old or so. The dad carried the youngest on his shoulders, getting snow from his boots down the front of his coat.

They were a loud yet fun-looking family.

After I personally welcomed them to Garland, the dad took a step closer, pulling out his wallet. "We'd like to place an order, please. A large order."

"Of course, sir. It would be my pleasure."

As I packed up their three dozen snowballs, I gave them my best tips and tricks for a snowball fight they'd never forget and told them where the best spot in town was to have it.

"And after you're done, make sure you stop by the Cocoa Corner. They've got the best hot cocoa in town, and it'll warm you right up."

"We rode the train!" The youngest exclaimed, bouncing on his dad's shoulders.

"You did?" I said, grinning up at the kid. "How exciting."

Customer service was everything. That was one thing I'd learned having a business. It's what made people come back.

That and great snowballs.

The family left, I couldn't help but think about seeing Bethany a few moments ago. It was the first time I'd seen her since Eli had asked me to look out for her.

I laughed to myself as I remembered her comment earlier. I didn't know her as well as I would've liked, but one thing I did know about her was that she was shy at times.

I loved seeing her get nervous, the way her eyelashes fluttered like she could blink away the world.

The way her lovely cheeks bloomed crimson red. And her long red hair. It just mesmerized me.

Despite the fact she refused to make eye contact after her comment, she seemed to be doing okay. Even more of a reason to keep my distance from her. Not because I wanted to, but because bro code dictated that I never get involved with her like that. Eli only wanted me to step in if she seemed lonely.

And how could she be when she was hanging out with the coolest grandma ever?

I got back to work, packing up more snowballs. My mind was almost off Bethany when I saw her exit The Nutcracker down the street. Alone. It was her shimmering red hair that caught my eye, even from down the block. Even under her hat. Even with hundreds of tourists milling about.

She was magnetic.

Before I could really think about it, I flipped my bright open sign to *Be Back Soon* and headed down the street toward Bethany.

What am I doing? I asked myself.

Keeping an eye on her. Like I'd promised Eli.

I was just making sure she was alright. Besides, I wouldn't talk to her. Just check on her.

How exactly I was supposed to do that without talking to her, I didn't know. Clearly, I hadn't thought this through.

Especially since I was still following her down the street. Stalling when she paused to look into a shop window, a wondrous look on her pretty face. Garland was so much better through her eyes. Even though I grew bored of the same attractions year after year, she interacted with them like they were all brand new.

I followed her for a little while, wondering in the back of my mind what it would be like to hold her hand or tuck her hair behind her ear. To comment on the bits and bobs with her.

It wasn't long before Bethany turned the corner

and walked into Cocoa Corner. I paused, staring at the door of the coffee shop.

I shouldn't go in.

I really shouldn't.

I pushed the door open and went in just in time to see Bethany take a seat at a booth and set down her bag next to her.

This was a bad idea. *A really bad idea*, I told myself. So I decided to leave and get back to my snowball stand before she could see what an idiot I was being.

Even though it felt wrong to not be near her.

What I would give to buy her a cup of hot cocoa and sit right next to her...

I pushed out the door just like I pushed away any feelings I'd had towards Bethany, but now that I had been asked to keep an eye on her, it felt impossible to keep denying that I had the biggest crush on her.

At the same time, though, I could never let something like this get in the way of my friendship with Eli. It would make things really weird at best. Completely ruin our friendship at worst.

You just didn't do that to your best friend. You'd date anyone else but their little sister.

I kicked a pile of snow out of my way as I walked back toward Cider Center.

One thing I hadn't thought about now that Eli was gone was how much less I'd see Bethany without hanging out at his house.

I liked hearing the sound of her voice. Hearing the sound of her sewing machine when we walked past her room. Greeting her and getting a smile in return.

"Hey," I heard behind me. It took me a second to realize I recognized the voice. The voice I'd just been thinking about.

I turned around slowly, and there she was. Just a few feet away and still walking toward me and tugging on her coat.

Even among the crowd of tourists, Bethany stood out like a goddess among men.

She continued walking until she came to a stop a few feet away from me. She put her hands on her hips. "Are you following me?"

"Following you?" Kane sputtered. His eyes widened, and for the first time maybe ever he looked nervous around me.

Something really was up with him.

"You heard me," I said, not sounding as confident as I'd hoped.

He relaxed the smallest amount and shrugged. "Why would I be following you?"

My eyes narrowed.

We stood face to face on the street, tourists walking past us and talking about where they were going next.

I ignored all of them to focus on Kane.

He had the warmest, honey-brown eyes, but I made myself not think about that.

He was hiding something, and I wanted to know what it was.

"I should get back to—" he began, pointing his thumb over his shoulder.

"Tell me what's really going on," I said, cutting him off with the no-nonsense voice I had to use on my brother from time to time.

He didn't say anything, but he also looked torn. A little guilty, even?

"I've never known you to be anything but honest," I pressed. "Is that going to change now?"

He took a step toward me, spreading his hands calmly. I noticed they were bare of the waterproof gloves he usually wore. "Okay, you caught me."

Aha. So I *had* been right. He was following me. But why? I gave him a questioning look.

"Eli asked me to look after you while he was gone. Make sure you were okay," he admitted, hanging his head so I got a good look at the top of his charcoal gray beanie.

It was impossible to know exactly how, but I knew he was telling the truth. It just wasn't what I was expecting to hear.

"*Eli* asked you to look after me?" I responded dumbly.

Kane tried to say something else, but I raised

CURVY ALL THE WAY

my hand. "But that's stupid. I don't need anyone looking out for me. I'm only a year younger than you guys!" This was just what I needed. Kane to see me as a child, someone who needed *babysitting*.

Kane looked kind of sheepish when I said that. "He's just protective of you, Bethany. That's all. He felt bad that you got left here on your own."

"I'm not on my own," I said, putting my hands on my hips. "I'm with my grandmother. And I'm working on finishing a very important project." He didn't need to treat me like a baby. "I could've gone, you know," I added. "But I chose not to." Because I was old enough to make my own choices!

Kane didn't say anything. Probably knew better.

"And besides, I can take care of myself. I don't need a boy to take care of me, even if it is you, Kane." Even if I had a huge crush on him.

He nodded, held up his hands again in self-defense. "You're right. You're completely right."

"Good," I replied. "So you'll stop following me around then?" Disappointment washed over me as I said that. I wanted to spend time with him, but not like this.

But Kane toed his snow boot over the sidewalk.

"I kind of promised your brother I'd watch out for you. I can't break a promise."

I turned back around slowly. My eyes locked with his.

"Please don't ask me to break my word to him," he asked gently.

Part of me was ready to chew him out a little bit more. But another part of me saw the kindness and sincerity in his eyes. His integrity was part of why I liked him.

And even though I didn't like how my brother had gone about doing this, it was nice enough to know he cared about me. That he wasn't just running off to tour colleges on the other coast and forgetting all about me.

I rolled my eyes, giving in. "Fine, but no more following me around." I turned to go back to Cocoa Corner where my drink was surely waiting, and Kane was beside me in a flash.

"Well, I have to check on you one way or another, don't I? How else am I going to keep my word?"

Now it was my turn to shrug. "Guess it's a mystery." I walked and he followed.

"Maybe I could spend time with you?" he suggested.

My heart skipped a beat at those words. At the possibility that maybe he would want to see me for a reason that had nothing to do with my older brother.

But I knew that wasn't the case. I put on a firm face as we walked down the sidewalk. "How much time are we talking? How much time to keep your word to my brother?"

"I don't know," he replied.

We continued walking down Main Street, and I realized this was the first time we had ever walked together, just the two of us.

I tried not to think about that too much.

"Just enough time to make sure the boogey man doesn't get me?" I asked him with some major side-eye.

That made him laugh.

His laugh was the best sound in the world to me. And it made me almost melt to know that I had been the one to make him laugh.

We paused outside Cocoa Corner, and sure enough, I could see my cocoa on the table, my bag still on the bench.

There was a tone of caution in his voice as Kane said, "Maybe I can check in with you every day? See what you're up to? Find out if you need anything?"

On the outside, I kept a poker face, but on the inside, I was thrilled at the thought of seeing Kane every day. Talking to him. Maybe pretending for a single week that he wasn't my brother's best friend. "I guess that would be acceptable. And if I need anything, then I guess you'll be the one I ask."

I wondered what he had to say to that.

"Okay," he said like it was no big deal.

"Even if it means you'll try on my designs so I can check measurements and made adjustments?" I gave him a quick up and down. "I actually have the perfect dress for you to help me with."

Kane groaned, and his shoulders sagged, but he was also kind of smiling. "Oh no, what am I signing up for?"

"That's the deal," I said with a grin. "Take it or leave it."

He straightened up. "Fine, fine, fine. I'll do it. Whatever you need in exchange for being able to check in with you."

"I guess we'll be spending some time together this week, then," I said, still doing my best to keep my poker face on.

"I guess we will," he said.

Even though I knew this was just him keeping his promise to Eli, I couldn't help but feel my stomach flutter at the thought of seeing Kane every day and having an excuse to talk to him.

"Well, you saw me today," I went on. "So I guess I'll see you tomorrow?"

"Tomorrow," he confirmed.

"Meet me at my grandmother's house on Gingerbread Lane when you're done working. You can help me with my sewing project."

"I'll be there," he said. "Just as soon as I close up shop for the day."

I thought of him in my runway dress. "Good," I said with a smile, and I finally turned toward home and left.

6
KANE

*S*o much for trying to be discreet while keeping my promise to Eli.

I hadn't gone more than one day—or even an hour—without Bethany figuring out that I was up to something. And I'd completely gone against my better judgement, agreeing to see her every day while Eli was gone.

Good thing I'd been born with some business skills because clearly, I was never going to make it as a hired private investigator.

Now I was on my way to their grandma's house thinking about all the ways this arrangement could go wrong. She knew the truth, which meant I wouldn't have to be a weirdo following her around, but I'd also be spending a lot more time with her... Possibly with just the two of us without her family around.

And that was the problem: I wasn't sure I trusted myself to be around her when it was just the two of us.

I imagined her sitting in front of the sewing machine, the determined look of hers pinching her eyebrows together. I could reach out and smooth the crease with my thumb. And when she looked up at me... I blinked hard, continuing down the sidewalk.

It could never happen.

I couldn't let it happen.

I was getting ahead of myself. Bethany didn't see me like that. I was the guy who was always hanging out with her brother. A dumb jock who sold snow in my free time. She had big goals that would surely take her away from Garland one day.

So, I needed to get over my feelings for her and keep things cool with her. Otherwise, I'd be in way more trouble than just getting caught following her.

On my way to Bethany's grandmother's house, I stopped by Stuffer's, our local grocery store. It was the only one around this small town and overflowing with food to keep up with tourist demand.

There weren't any big stores or supermarkets around here. Everything was local and unique to us. Not to mention, Christmas-themed.

But we didn't lack at all. Especially considering Stuffer's carried the best pastries, pies, and other baked goods, made fresh every day.

I walked in and made my way over to the bakery section. The cinnamon scent from fresh cookies was making my mouth water. I knew for a fact from their baking schedule that Bethany's favorite ginger snaps and iced cookies had just been made.

I also knew that her favorite color was green. All sorts of shades of green. I'd overheard her say that once.

The sound of a baby crying nearby brought me back down to Earth.

I found the cookies and made my way to the register with the white box in my hand.

The upside of being a successful small business owner in Garland was always having cash on me. Certainly enough cash to take a nice girl on a very nice date. But I'd never taken any girl on any date because the one girl I wanted I could never have. At least I could get her cookies.

I checked out and headed out the door in time

to see where the crying had come from. A mom shushed her baby sitting in the cart while her toddler sat in the bigger basket and an older kid followed behind her. They lived in Garland and had used my stand several times.

"It's okay, baby," the mom said, looking to be on the verge of tears herself.

"Make sure you stop by the snowball stand tomorrow, okay?" I gave the older kid a fist bump. "There's a jumbo size basket of snowballs with your name on it. On the house."

He grinned and his toddler sister clapped her hands together. The baby was so distracted, the tears stopped for a minute. Their mom thanked me profusely. "They are going to take the best nap tomorrow after they're done playing," she said. Her eyes gleamed with the tears of a woman who could use a quiet afternoon.

"No need to thank me," I said, meaning it. It was just snow. And I loved this time of year–least I could do is make it fun for the neighborhood kids.

It was important to give back. Sometimes that meant all-you-could-throw snowballs for a family who could use some fun. And sometimes it meant making a donation to Santa's Elves so families going through a tough time could have a good Christmas.

When I got to Bethany's grandmother's house, I had quite a bit of snow to shake off of my coat before stepping inside. My hands were cold, but luckily the cookies were still warm in their box.

"Oh my goodness, thank you!" Mrs. Hart said. "These are Bethany's favorite."

"I hope you both enjoy them," I said as she took the cookies and I hung my coat.

I followed her to the craft room, where Bethany sat in front of a large, light blue sewing machine. It was loud, and I saw her foot pressing down firmly on the pedal, her brows stitched together in concentration as she pushed fabric through the machine.

I wondered if this was the dress she'd been telling me about.

Her gaze shifted to me, and she took her foot off the petal, silencing the machine to a quiet hum.

I gave her a small wave. "Hey, sorry to interrupt."

"Kane," she said like her mind was still on her project. "Hi."

"Can I get you anything?" Mrs. Hart asked me. I'd almost forgotten she was here while watching

Bethany. "I'm great, Mrs. Hart, thank you." She nodded and left.

I moved closer to Bethany and took a seat on a faded red padded chair in the corner of the room. "Is this the infamous dress?" It was long and green with different types of fabric. I wished I could see more of it, but it was hard to see very much of it with all the fabric scrunched together.

"It is," she said with a devilish grin on her face. "I really think it's your color."

"It might not pass the school dress code," I said with a chuckle.

She laughed, and she pulled out the dress from the sewing machine. "It is strapless." She held it up then, analyzing it–for what, I wasn't sure. The dress already looked perfect–I could picture her in it at prom, dancing with me.

"Are you almost done?" I asked to distract myself from that line of thinking.

She blew a slow stream of air from her mouth. "I wish." She turned the dress around and inspected a seam. "I've got a long way to go on this if it's going to be anywhere near good enough to land me a spot in the program I want to get into. Even the tiniest details have to be perfect."

I looked around the room. It looked like she'd

41

brought all her sewing stuff over from her house. After years of hanging out with Eli, I'd gotten familiar with Bethany and her sewing. "How'd you get into sewing and fashion and all of this?"

I realized I'd never asked her. Or even heard her talk about it, but I knew there had to be a reason. No one was this passionate about something without having a motive.

The second Bethany's cheeks flushed red and she shifted uncomfortably in her chair, I immediately regretted asking the question. It must have been highly personal to her.

"Sorry," I said quickly. "I didn't mean to pry. I mean, it's none of my business—"

"It's okay," she said, setting the dress down on the table in front of her. "I guess I need to get good at explaining it to people. If I get into that program, then I'll be doing it a lot more."

She paused, and I waited for her to gather her thoughts. Her amber eyes met mine like she was ready to talk.

"I guess I fell in love with fashion because it's really hard to feel beautiful when you're shopping old styles on a tiny plus-size rack at the back of the store because none of the regular clothes fit you." She glanced toward the floor, her cheeks still flushed, but she kept going. "All women deserve to feel beautiful. We deserve to have options and be able to express ourselves with our clothes like anyone else."

I wanted to say something, but I also didn't want to blurt out something stupid after how vulnerable she'd just been with me. I'd never had to think much about clothes–you go to the store, grab your size off the rack, and bring them home. But clearly it wasn't like that for Bethany.

Anger rose up in my chest that clothing stores had made her feel unattractive, because the girl across from me? She was *stunning*.

I stood up and without letting myself think too much about it, I tucked a stray strand of hair behind her ear. "Whatever you do, Bethany, never question how beautiful you are. I mean it."

Our eyes locked for a second, and before I could say anything else, she glanced away. I took that as my queue to back off. What had I been thinking?

I took a seat back in the chair I'd been in, hoping she wouldn't tell Eli I overstepped.

"So," Bethany said quickly. "Tell me about you. What are you up to these days? I mean, besides the snowball stand. What's in your future?"

It felt like we were solidly back in friendly territory, and we were staying there, for sure. "I want to play baseball in college–like your brother– but more than that, I want to have a career as a coach."

We talked like that for a while. Bethany would hand stitch on her dress for a few minutes and when she got back to the machine, the sound of it running would make it impossible to talk. Then she'd stop for a minute to check her work and we'd talk again.

Before I knew it, it was getting late. The street-lights shined brightly outside the window, along with the neighbor's Christmas lights and decorations. It was time for me to go.

I'd risked enough already.

Even so, I said, "Check in again tomorrow?"

"Okay," she said with a small smile that made me far more hopeful than I had any right to be. "Thanks for keeping me company."

"Just doing my job," I quipped as I left, still thinking about that smile and how close I'd come to kissing her.

7
BETHANY

ane was a distracting guy.

Not because he tried to be. No, he sat quietly beside me most of the time yesterday, only talking when I asked him a question or when I wasn't actively using the sewing machine.

His presence was, though. He had this intoxicating cologne that smelled like the air right before it started snowing. His voice was low and smooth, making my stomach erupt with butterflies every time he spoke. And his eyes? I felt like they saw right through me.

I needed to stop thinking about Kane and focus solely on the application since the deadline was just a few days away.

Luckily, I had sewing club to keep me on track. Because of the holidays, we were meeting most days.

Grandma helped me pack up my things and we walked there together. I hugged my tote bag with my design book close to my chest, making sure the snow didn't get to it while she pulled her weatherproof cart along the salt-covered sidewalk.

When we walked inside the room off to the side of Vixen's Salon, the ladies were abuzz, catching up, even though they'd just seen each other the other day.

We found our usual seats and sat down.

Everyone was working on Christmas gifts for loved ones, from blankets to embroidered tea towels. But I was working on over a dozen designs still far from perfect.

The application instructions said they were more concerned with our designs than sewing skills, but I wanted my application to stand out. Just like most plus-size women needed to try on clothes to get the full effect, the judges would need to see my garments to truly see how special they were.

All of my pieces could probably work except

the formal design. I hadn't perfected it yet, and it had me stressed out.

I told the ladies all about my many attempts sewing and ripping apart the seams while we worked around a big round table. "It all feels hopeless. I follow the program's hashtag online, and someone applied with these couture designs I couldn't even dream of creating. At first, I thought my stitchwork would set me apart, but I'm worried it won't be enough."

Mrs. Cole kept her eyes on the needle she was trying to thread as she said, "You're not going to change your designs, are you? They're darling." With the needle threaded, she held it up to drive her point home.

The rest of the ladies *hmphed* and nodded in agreement.

"We have to go with your gut about the stitching not being enough," Mrs. Patty said, putting her project down. "The judges would have to be looking really close to notice, and it sounds like they'll have a lot of designs to get through."

Mrs. Katz had a worried look on her heavily made-up face as she said, "There's got to be something else you can do to make a splash with your application aside from your designs and technical skills. We can show that other people love your designs too. The judges have to like designs that have garnered attention."

"You know," Mrs. Mulberry said, hands stilling over the massive quilt on her lap. "The most successful fundraiser we ever did for Santa's Elves was a fashion show."

My ears perked up. I've loved fashion shows ever since I was a little girl. I watched them on TV, begged my parents to take me to them in person, and even put on fashion shows of my own with each new design.

"What if we put on a fashion show?" Grandma suggested. "Of all your designs."

I nodded excitedly, envisioning it so clearly in my eyes. "I could include the video of it in my application. A simple QR code is all I would need."

"A what now?" Mrs. Cole said. "Is that what my grandkids can never connect to when they come over?"

I laughed. "No, that's the Wi-Fi, Mrs. Cole. A QR code is…" I stopped, deflating with each second that passed as I realized that a fashion show would never actually work. "Never mind. It's great idea, but there's no way I have enough time to put together an entire fashion show *and* finish the hand stitching."

"Not you putting on the show, hon," Grandma said. "Us." She waved her hands around the ladies in the circle.

"That's right," Mrs. Katz said with a determined nod, and pretty soon everyone chimed in saying they'd help.

My heart swelled with how willing they were to help me. I felt a little guilty by all they were willing to do for me. "Christmas is next week," I pointed out. "I'm sure all of you have plenty of things to do without—"

Mrs. Katz got up and walked over to me. She put her beautifully manicured hand on my shoulder, and I finally stopped talking. "You can count on us, dear."

"Besides," Mrs. Mulberry said with a wink. "We know all the tricks of the trade."

A sense of wonder washed over me as I looked around at all of the sewing ladies. Was this really happening?

They seemed to be waiting for me to say something, so I gave them a tentative smile, allowing myself to be hopeful. This really could be the thing that got me into the program. "Okay, let's do it!"

They began clapping, and you'd think I'd just announced that Christmas was now happening twice a year instead of once. They seemed even more excited than me.

And technically, I wouldn't be breaking any rules. The designs were all mine. They'd just be helping me display them.

"If you finish your designs by Christmas Eve, then we can have the fashion show the day after Christmas," my grandmother said.

I nodded, thinking I could make it by then. But another question popped into my head. "Where could we have the fashion show?" I asked.

Nothing was coming to mind. No one else chimed in either. Every place that would be worthwhile had probably been booked for months with this being the height of the tourism season.

"I'll figure it out," I said. "Don't worry. You ladies take care of the details. And I'll find a place."

8

KANE

I hadn't seen Bethany around Cider Center all day, which disappointed me more than it had any right to. I knew she had to be busy with her application, but I liked seeing her out and about. She always wore a brightly colored coat, and her stocking hats had all different designs like she was determined to show off her fashion sense even in the winter when we had to be all bundled up.

At least this time of year was busy for my business. I didn't have much time to sit and stew on my thoughts when person after person were coming to my kiosk to purchase a set of snowballs.

After packaging up a couple dozen snowballs

for some middle schoolers and then another dozen for the parents of a preschooler, I pulled out my phone from my pocket.

Since there was a short lull of customers, I took off my gloves, wondering what Bethany was up to today. It wasn't against the rules to text her, right? I just couldn't follow her. Or date her.

So I shot her a text and pulled my gloves back on.

It wasn't long before my phone dinged in response.

I had to fulfill another order before checking her response.

Bethany: Hey there. Pretty busy.

That wasn't a surprise. She might have been nervous about this application, but I knew she'd get in. She was going to make it big one day as a designer. I could feel it in my bones like I felt the cold winter air every day in this small town. I had a cool side hustle and great customers. But Bethany? She had a dream of changing the world. That made all the difference.

I thought about what to text her back, what to

say to have an excuse to see her. Maybe even make her day better with the stress she was under.

Kane: How about taking a break to do something fun?

It wasn't long before she replied.

Bethany: I don't think so. No time. Lots to do.

I believed her. But one thing I also knew about hard work? Sometimes it helped to step away and recharge for a bit.

Kane: Listen, before you know it, Christmas will be over. You deserve to enjoy it at least a little before that happens, don't you think?

I saw little bubbles pop up on my screen. Then disappear. Then reappear once more.

I was ready to present my best argument to her, which is why I was surprised when her message came through.

Bethany: Maybe you're right. What did you have in mind?

I grinned.

Kane: How about a movie?

More text bubbles.

Bethany: With popcorn?

Kane: You know it.

She hearted my message.
Then sent a screenshot of the movie schedule.

Bethany: My favorite movie is playing at 5!

It was *The Holiday*. I cringed, thinking of the time my mom made us watch it as a family. She had kept going on about how handsome Jude Law was even after it ended. Probably wouldn't have been my pick, but hey, I would be sitting next to Bethany for two hours, so it couldn't be that bad.

Bethany: Too cheesy?

I wanted to say yes, but I didn't care what we

were watching so long as I got to spend time with her.

Kane: Not at all, I'll see you there.

I let out a breath. I wanted to punch the air in victory, like when the pretty girl you ask out says yes.

But this wasn't a date. I had to keep reminding myself of that. This was just me being a good friend. Me checking in on her during the holidays while her family was out of town.

I was telling myself the same thing over and over again at A Wonderful Film when I walked in a couple hours later. But I wanted it to be a date when I saw Bethany arrive in a deep green sweater dress with a thick, golden scarf woven through with shiny threads. It brought out her eyes and contrasted her hair beautifully.

I had to keep my hands from shaking as I paid for our tickets and the popcorn, even though she tried to argue. And when the lights turned down and a bucket of popcorn sat in my lap, I could smell her perfume. It smelled like peppermint, sugar, and cinnamon all mixed together. Different than that cotton candy perfume she got when we were eleven and ten. Her brother had pretended to faint she sprayed so much of it in the air.

Things were different now.

Way different.

It was just the two of us in the movie theater, and I would've given anything just to hold Bethany's hand.

It was like torture sitting this close to her and not being able to put my arm around her.

Whatever perfume she was wearing wasn't helping. She smelled like the best parts of Christmas, and all I wanted to do was find out if her mouth tasted just as sweet.

By the time the movie was over, I was relieved. It took all my willpower to keep from closing the two-inch gap between our fingers and hold her hand.

The more I spent time with Bethany, the more my feelings for her solidified and grew. I'd always thought that maybe I just had a crush on her, part of being around her all the time. Now I could see it was more than that. My whole body practically screamed *DUH* in agreement.

We tossed our empty popcorn buckets and left the movies, walking in the direction of Bethany's grandmother's house. It was dark out now, and even though it hadn't snowed all day, tiny snowflakes began falling from the sky as we made our way home.

Not only that, but Christmas lights twinkled all around us, making Garland feel even more magical than it did the rest of the year.

A couple walked by us, arm in arm, and a twinge of jealousy filled my chest.

A split second later, Bethany shrieked, and I instinctively stuck my arms out to grab her. She had slipped on some ice on the sidewalk.

"Oh my gosh," she breathed, looking up at me. Her eyes sparkled back up at me. "Thank you."

Was it me or was she glancing at my lips? In a flash, I was doing the same. Then, as fast as she'd fallen, the moment was over. She stood up, but I didn't let go until I was sure she was steady on her feet again. "Are you okay?" I asked, my voice almost a whisper.

"Yeah, thanks to you," she said with a breathy chuckle. "How'd you even react that fast?"

I grinned at the compliment. "I don't even know, but I'm glad I did."

Our eyes met again, but this time, Bethany looked away.

Was it me, or had things become awkward between us in the last few seconds?

"So, what about the application is keeping you busy?" I asked, trying to change the subject as we began walking again.

"Well," she told me. "It's turned into a whole fashion show."

"What?" I said with a small laugh. "How'd you create more work for yourself?"

She laughed at that, and I was glad.

"I really want my application to stand out, so I'm going to have real women model my designs."

"That sounds really cool," I replied.

"Yeah, I'm excited, even if it feels impossible to put it all together. But the sewing club promised to help me out with that. And I'm working on finding somewhere to host it." She looked stumped as she said the last part.

"What can I do to help?" I asked.

She turned to me. "I couldn't ask you to do that. It's your busy season too."

"Sure you can," I said, and we stopped walking, at an impasse.

She didn't say anything for a second. "Would it be for me or my brother?"

I locked eyes with her. Something about how

she said it made me want to tell her the truth about my feelings. But I knew I couldn't do that without betraying Eli's trust.

So instead, I brushed her hair back behind her ear and grinned. "Don't ask questions you know I can't answer."

We kept walking, and I stuck my hands in my pockets... to keep from reaching for hers.

9

BETHANY

I woke up the next morning with Kane on my mind. He was on my mind a lot these days, more than ever before. What had always been more of an impossible schoolgirl crush to me before... was now somehow feeling like a real possibility.

His words from last night played over and over in my mind.

"Don't ask questions you know I can't answer."

My stomach fluttered at the memory and the look in his eyes.

I don't even know what had prompted me to ask him if he was helping me for me or my brother. Kane had been so close to me, and clearly, I wasn't thinking clearly. I had just blurted it out.

But his answer had caught me completely off guard. The way his fingers had tucked my hair behind my ear? I had practically floated away on a cloud. How I'd managed to remember to use my legs to keep walking home, I had no idea.

I had never expected that kind of gesture from Kane, but now that my brother and parents were away, it was like we had a few precious days to forget that we could never be a thing.

Well, maybe not "we," but me.

I couldn't forget how close his face had been to mine, though.

I rolled over in bed and remembered how good Kane had smelled. Like fresh snow and cinnamon rolls.

My phone dinged, bringing me back down to earth.

I rubbed the sleep from my eyes and checked the notification.

I sat up immediately. It was an email from the fashion school I was applying to. If I got in, I'd be going there all summer to work with some of the biggest names in fashion. They'd give me feedback and direction with my designs. Maybe even open doors for college, internships, or actual jobs in fashion design. From there, the possibilities were limitless.

But it all started with getting into this program.

And now, an email from them sat in my inbox reminding me that the application was due in less than week.

I got out of bed and began getting ready for the day at double speed. As much as I wanted to spend the day in bed, finally catching up on sleep and maybe daydreaming about Kane, I couldn't.

The deadline for my application was right around the corner, and it wasn't nearly perfected enough to secure my spot in the program.

I couldn't put a boy above my dreams, even if it was Kane.

I would never forgive myself.

Determined to do better, I stared back at myself in the mirror and reminded myself that I couldn't let my feelings for him get in the way of making this the best fashion show ever to aid my application.

I got dressed, thinking instead of the things I still needed to do to get my designs ready for a real-life fashion show.

Part of me wondered if I'd been hasty to agree to one so last minute, but my gut said it was the right move to stand out among a sea of applicants who wanted a spot at least as bad as I did. Each year, they averaged thousands of applicants and only accepted ten. I wanted one of those spots so bad I could taste it.

So I doubled down, working on the dress so it would be ready for its grand debut.

This was one of my favorite parts of perfecting a design–that I could get completely lost in my work, unaware of how much time had passed, let alone the world around me.

I had done just so when my phone went off with a ding, causing me to jump, pricking myself with a needle. As I drew my finger to my lips, I glanced at the phone. Several hours had passed. And I'd gotten a text from Kane.

Kane: Meet me at the diner for lunch? And before you can argue, let me remind you that you *do* have to eat to survive.

Now that he mentioned food, my stomach growled. I'd skipped breakfast in my rush to get to work. I texted him back that I would meet him, giving myself the condition that I needed to set aside how I felt about him and focus on the fashion show.

I shrugged on my bright-pink coat with a

matching pink and gray stocking cap and scarf, then started toward Scrooge's Diner.

It was the one business in Garland that refused to celebrate Christmas, with the same art on the walls and lack of Christmas lights all year long. The guy who owned it hated Christmas and kicked out anyone who spoke of it in the diner. Everyone called him Scrooge, and the mayor even argued with him every year to add at least a little decoration, but his food was the best in town.

Eager for a good meal, I walked into the diner with my design book and the plans and notes I had so far for the fashion show.

The ladies at the sewing club were organizing the event, but I had to figure out the fashion show itself, and there were way more logistics than I had anticipated. Music, the design order, and the customary speech a designer gave at each show.

I pushed into the diner, a bell chiming against the wood and glass door. Kane grinned up at me so warmly, my knees went weak. I gathered my resolve as I approached him at the small booth in the corner. He'd already ordered a drink.

"Hi, Kane," I said. He went in for a hug, and I made it quick before sitting down. (Hey, a girl could only withstand so much!)

I avoided his mesmerizing eyes, staring at the menu instead. Thankfully, Scrooge distracted me further by showing up to take my drink order.

After ordering a soda, he left, and it was just Kane and me again.

"I just wanted to say thanks for being willing to help me with all this," I said, laying out my stuff.

"You don't have to thank me," Kane said, looking at the plans I had. "I'm happy to do what I can."

His smile was infectious. His eyes gleamed, and it was all I could do not to get lost in them. I cleared my throat and explained what I had planned already, which wasn't much, and how much there was left to consider. "The main thing is I still need a location to have the fashion show. Then I'll need to come up with a schedule to showcase the designs and what I'll say about each one."

I was going a million miles per hour while he was looking at all of my fashion designs. "You created all of this?" he asked, holding up a design of a long dress he hadn't see yet.

"Yeah, I did," I said. "That's the reason for the fashion show," I teased.

He looked impressed. "I always knew you were talented, but I didn't realize how good you were at this," he said. He picked up another design, this one of a pair of trousers and a long-sleeve top. "I have no idea about fashion, and even I can tell this is good. You've got a real gift, Bethany."

I felt my face turn hot, and I glanced down. "Thanks, Kane." I summoned the courage to meet his eyes. "That means a lot coming from you." Especially since I thought he barely knew I existed.

He smiled, and butterflies rose from my stomach. "You're going to win this thing. I just know it."

I laughed, because it wasn't really a win or lose situation, but I got what he meant.

Scrooge arrived with my soda, and Kane let him know we needed a few minutes before we would be ready to order.

Scrooge left, muttering under his breath about people thinking his diner was a workspace.

Kane chuckled. "Don't worry. We'll leave him a good tip." He picked up my notes and looked at me. "But first, I have an idea for the location."

*B*ethany had told me about all the places she'd thought of and struck out with when it came to hosting her fashion show since it was so last minute. The way she explained things, it seemed like if she could figure out that part of it, then the rest of the show had a really good chance of coming together thanks to the ladies in her sewing club.

I didn't know much when it came to fashion, but one thing I *could* do was call in a favor.

Every holiday season, I gifted the baseball coach's family all-you-can-throw snowballs as a thanks for investing in me each season. And he had four kids, so it was a *lot* of snowballs. And a lot of fun memories.

So when I called and asked him if there was any way we could use the stage at the school for Bethany's fashion show, he immediately said yes.

Now, Bethany and I were taking a quick inventory of the stage at the school while snow fell softly through the night sky outside. We walked in through the double doors to the large auditorium.

I had guessed that it would be perfect for what she needed, and judging by the look on her face, I had been right.

Grinning from ear to ear, Bethany ran past me to the stage and then turned to me in amazement. "I can't believe you got the school to let us use the stage! It's always completely shut down over Christmas!"

I grinned, loving how she had lit up like the tree in Cider Center. "Merry Christmas."

Bethany glanced around at the many rows of seats. "We'll definitely be able to invite plenty of people, which will be perfect."

I walked further into the auditorium, going down the sloped aisle toward her. "Coach Miller let me know there's a runway extension we can set up, if we promise to put it all back when we're done."

That made Bethany shriek and jump up and

down. "We'll have a catwalk?! This is great! I can already envision the show. We'll have seats here and here," she said, pointing to different areas near the stage. "And the music... I need to put together a playlist!"

She turned to me. "What about dressing rooms? We'll need dressing rooms nearby for the models to change quickly."

I motioned for her to follow me backstage. "I've got it covered. Come on. I'll show you."

I led her up the steps to the stage then behind the curtains. There were several dressing rooms back there with plenty of privacy that the theater kids used for musicals. And a separate entrance so models wouldn't have to go past the general audience to get inside.

"Oh, this will be so convenient," she said, walking into the dressing room area. I went in behind her. There were several curtained off dressing rooms with mirrors and tables for doing makeup.

I could see she was ready to keep looking around, so I turned back toward the door, realizing it had closed behind me.

I turned the doorknob, but the door wouldn't open.

Looking back at Bethany, I realized just how alone we were in this space. She looked so pretty, her cheeks all pink with excitement, her brain obviously going wild with her plans. My hands itched to touch her. To kiss her.

But she said, "Are we stuck in here?"

Reality came crashing back, and I returned my attention to the door.

After rattling it a few times, the latch or lock or whatever finally unlocked and the door opened. "Sorry about that," I told Bethany. "Coach told me this door was finicky. Maintenance is supposed to fix it after the holidays."

"I still think it's perfect," Bethany said, as I allowed her to exit before me. I could smell her perfume as she passed.

"I think so, too," I replied, letting the door close gently behind me.

We explored more of the backstage area—the part we couldn't accidentally get locked inside—and Bethany explained all sorts of things about the fashion show that I could barely keep up with.

Her passion for it was as easy to see as her bright-pink coat. She was going to make a name for herself soon. That much was evident to me.

This fashion show would be the beginning of

her upward trajectory, and I was just grateful to play a small part in it.

"What?" Bethany said, looking at me.

I blinked a few times, realizing I'd been staring at her silently for a little too long. "Nothing," I said. "Just thinking about how good this is all working out." I began walking toward a room at the other side of the stage. "Let me show you the props and supplies storage that Coach Miller showed me. I think some of it will come in handy."

We went through the large supply and prop room, pulling out things Bethany could use for the fashion show. I grabbed a bucket of white paint. "I'm thinking we could customize some of these props according to your designs."

"Like a theme," Bethany said.

"Sure," I said, not completely sure what she meant, but glad to see she was already coming up with ideas to match her vision.

After going through all the props, we finally went back out to the stage. I sat down at the edge, letting my feet dangle off the side and Bethany did the same. Our shoulders were nearly touching. Just a couple inches away.

She stared out at the auditorium in silence, and I could tell she was deep in thought.

"What's on your mind?" I asked quietly.

She turned toward me, and I was surprised to see tears in her eyes. "Honestly? I'm just really happy we got this stage."

I smiled, glad they were happy tears. "Me too."

"I've got you to thank for that," she said, putting her hand on mine between us.

Warmth sparked from her touch, radiating all the way up my arm and flaring in my chest. "No thanks is necessary," I told her. And I meant it. I would do whatever it took to make Bethany happy.

To make her dreams come true.

She'd already put in so much hard work–I wasn't going to let the lack of a location for her fashion show stop her.

She moved her hand back to her lap, and I saw her smile disappear. "But now I'm worried I'm not going to be able to make this happen in time. Or that it won't be good enough if I do." Her voice cracked as she said it, and I fought the urge to immediately wrap my arms around her.

So instead, I put my hand on her shoulder.

She exhaled, her breath shaky. "My parents are gone. All of my friends are busy with stuff of their own." She turned to me, and I saw a tear roll down her cheek. "What if I can't pull this off by the deadline? What if I don't get in?"

I used my thumb to wipe away her tear. "Oh, you'll pull this off, don't you worry," I told her. "You're going to make this happen."

"You really think so?" she asked, sounding a little more hopeful.

I squeezed her shoulder. "I know so. And I'll be here to help you every step of the way."

11

BETHANY

The next day, I met up with Kane at the school after he sold out of snowballs. There was so much to do, and the good thing about his promise to my brother was that now I had his help every day until the day of the fashion show.

That's why he was helping me–it had to be.

Between Kane and the ladies at the sewing club, I was starting to feel more hopeful about my chances of getting in.

I felt a fresh buzz of energy as we got out the paint and the rest of the supplies to update the props. I'd decided on a winter wonderland theme for the fashion show. It would be perfect for the designs I was submitting. Having the town of

Garland as my inspiration, most of them were winter or holiday themed. A lot of the props were already here; they just needed updating to the right color.

Kane and I got to work making giant snowflakes in all shades of silver with sparkles on top. By the time we hung them up, the entire auditorium felt truly magical.

The best part of it was doing it all with Kane. The time flew by because I was having the best time with him. With my brother always around, we'd never had time by ourselves like this to really talk and get to know each other.

Best of all, Kane made me feel... I wasn't sure what the word was exactly. Maybe like I mattered? And not just in the "I'm your mom so I have to care about you" kind of way. Kane didn't have to say the supportive things he did. He'd more than fulfilled his promise to my brother. But he still acted like he cared about me.

As we worked on standing props for the stage, he asked me, "So when's the first time you thought fashion might be for you? When did you think, 'Hey, I think this is my thing'?"

I continued painting the backdrop while I mulled it over. I was on one end with a big paintbrush while Kane stood at the other, holding a brush and paint bucket of his own.

I liked how he didn't fill the silence while I thought of my answer. And when I started talking, I could see his brush stall on the prop like he really wanted to listen.

"I was in a dance competition ages ago," I began. "I must have been... nine or ten years old? And I couldn't find a costume in my size."

My cheeks heated at the admission. I had to admit it was a little weird to be telling Kane about this, since I'd only ever really talked about it with my friends, but I felt safe doing so now. "None of the 'regular-sized' costumes fit me. It was really upsetting. My dance teacher said maybe I could just wear black shorts and a tank top for the dance since I'd worked so hard to learn it. But I knew wearing a different outfit would make me feel even more out of place. I told Mom that I wanted to quit dancing."

Kane frowned. "That must have been hard, Beth. I'm sorry."

My lips tilted with gratitude. "It was hard. But my mom didn't want me to quit. She deserved my moment on stage just like all the other girls. So she and Grandma worked together after I went to bed to sew me a costume from scratch that looked just like all the other girls'. And it was the most beautiful thing I'd ever worn. They told me they found one at the store. It wasn't until a year or two later, when Grandma was giving me sewing lessons, that I found the scrap fabric from the costume and realized they had made it for me."

Kane smiled at that, I realized I was smiling, too. I'd felt so relieved and *normal* when I thought they'd just misplaced my costume at the store. But then I felt so loved they went to that effort for me.

"She was teaching me to sew blankets and pillows–things like that. I don't know why I'd never realized before that you could make and design your own clothes. I always thought the only choices you had were at the store. If something didn't fit or only big frumpy clothes were all they had in your size, then you were out of luck."

I kept painting and talking. "I wanted to make all of my own clothes after that." I chuckled. "Little did I know, there's a lot that goes into it. You should've seen the very first stuff I made. It was *not* good."

Kane laughed with me at that. "I remember that pillowcase dress you made. You wore it all summer long."

My cheeks heated, realizing that he had noticed me, even back then. Shaking off my blush, I continued. "Designing and sewing clothes that fit had made such a difference for me. To me, fashion isn't just about what's shown on magazine covers. It's tied to so much more, like your self-esteem and how you express yourself. Every girl deserves to feel special in what she wears, not just up to a size twelve."

"Wow," Kane said, a look of awe in his expression. "It's cool that you're doing something to make it better. Most people just accept sucky things are a part of life."

I smiled, blushing a little. "I don't know. I just… want to make plus-size girls like me feel beautiful. It's not something we get to feel very often."

That's when Kane put down his paintbrush and walked over to me. My heart skipped a beat as he walked right up to me.

What was he about to do?

He grinned as he looked down at me. My eyelashes fluttered as I realized how close he was to me. His nose was just inches from mine.

His hand reached up and picked something off my cheek. "You've got a sparkle on your cheek," he said softly and with a smile.

I was speechless. All I could do was look up at him, waiting for what would happen next.

"It's no match for the sparkle in your eyes, though," Kane said.

Was it me or was his face coming ever closer to mine?

My breath hitched as the side of his nose touched mine. The smell of cinnamon was wonderful. My eyes fluttered closed as I realized what was about to happen.

Then my phone began buzzing loudly. Loud enough to bring the moment between us crashing down.

I jumped back, and so did Kane.

I grabbed my phone from my pocket, wishing I could go back in time to just a minute ago.

But the magic was now over.

"Sorry," I told Kane, holding up my phone. "It's my mom."

I walked past him, down the steps, and off the stage. I took her call, careful not to glance back at Kane.

I didn't want to know if he was just as disappointed as me.

Or, maybe just embarrassed, even regretful.

I didn't want to think about it.

As my mom checked in on me and then told me all about my brother's trip and college visit, I couldn't help but think that I had let things go too far. I had lost focus on what mattered most.

I couldn't let something like that happen again.

12
KANE

*A*s I made my way home under the glow of all the Christmas lights on Candy Cane Lane, I couldn't help but feel a giant pit in my stomach over what had almost happened.

Bethany had been talking about her insecurities, and I wanted to yell from the freaking rooftops that she had no need to doubt herself. She was *gorgeous*. I noticed her any time she walked into a room. And it wasn't just her looks; it was the way she carried herself. She was so determined that it made me feel like I could chase my own goals too.

The words had been on the tip of my tongue. Bethany's lips had been less than an inch from mine. I had almost felt them on mine. And I didn't want to think about what would've happened if her mom hadn't called in that moment. I would have told her exactly how I felt about her. And the guilt I had now would've been multiplied by about a thousand.

Eli was my *best friend*. And I had almost betrayed him.

It didn't matter if my feelings for Bethany were sincere. Best friends would never do that to each other. Not behind his back like I'd almost done.

I kept my head down as I walked past the Caroling Karens singing "Silent Night" in front of a couple on their front porch. We were less than a week away from Christmas. This was prime time for them. But as nicely as the gossipy group of ladies sang, my mood was in the dumps.

When I got home and made it to my room, my phone buzzed with a text from Eli. It wasn't long before he was Face Timing me and telling me all about the college he was visiting.

He couldn't stop raving about it. He said the facilities were top notch and there was even a special dining hall just for student athletes.

"It sounds like a great school," I told him, forcing a smile to my face. "They'd be lucky to have you."

"Thanks, man," he said. "How's Bethany, by the way?"

I coughed but tried to clear my throat. "Good, she's good." Could he tell I was off? I didn't know what else to say without sounding like a fool or like I was hiding something.

I just prayed Eli would change the subject. But he didn't. "Well, don't go falling in love with my little sister while I'm gone," he joked. "That would be so weird."

I tried to laugh with him, but it was impossible. "Never, man. I wouldn't dream of it."

After that, Eli did change the subject, but the knot in my stomach only grew tighter.

What kind of friend was I?

THE NEXT MORNING, I was up bright and early to prep for work. I had a big batch of snowballs to get ready before I could open up shop. Hopefully some hard work would take my mind off of Bethany and what had almost transpired between us.

It took all of fifteen minutes to realize that wasn't going to happen. No matter how hard I shoveled snow or how many dozens of snowballs I made, I couldn't stop thinking about her.

Which only made me feel crummier than I already did.

Eli asking me to look after her was going to ruin our friendship for good.

And it was all my fault. Here she was, trying to focus on her application, and I couldn't stop thinking about how pretty she was and how much I liked spending time with her.

I was so deep in thought that I almost didn't notice Bethany walking by on the sidewalk.

She had a big pile of fabric in her arms, the kind you buy at the craft store by the yard.

She saw me at the same time I saw her, and she stopped. "Kane," she said.

"Bethany, what's up?" I said over the unsettled feeling in my chest.

She walked over, and I was torn between my guilt and being happy to see her. Bethany put down her pile of fabric on a bench nearby and moved toward the giant mountain of snow I still had left to turn into snowballs. "Let me help you."

I waved her off though. "It's okay. Don't worry about it. You've got enough on your plate."

But she didn't listen. Instead, she grabbed some

snow in her gloved hands and began forming a ball. "It's the least I can do. I owe you."

She hadn't quite met my eyes, and I hadn't quite met hers. But despite the awkwardness between us, I liked being close to her. I went back to making snowballs and noticed how much faster the work was going with her help. "You know, you don't owe me. Me helping you with the fashion show... that's just called being there for a friend."

I hoped she didn't cringe at the word "friend" like I had.

She kept making more snowballs, her expression unreadable. "I didn't mean the fashion show," she said. That made me look up at her in surprise. "If it weren't for you, I would have gotten picked on so bad during freshman year."

I looked at her, puzzled. I didn't remember doing anything to rescue her. In fact, I didn't remember Bethany getting picked on at all.

She explained, "My first day of freshman year, I walked in thinking I was hot stuff because I was wearing one of my designs. A skirt with this cute striped pattern." Even though she was looking at the packed snow in her hands, I could tell she was picturing the skirt in her mind. "Well, this girl, a senior, came up to me and asked if the local circus had lost one of their tents."

I groaned. "She didn't." Anger made me grip the snowball in my hands too tightly and it fell apart.

"Oh, she did," Bethany said. "I was mortified. I thought it had been a cute skirt, and she had just come along and... anyway, everyone was still laughing when you came up to me and put your hand on my shoulder."

She smiled. "You said hi to me and asked if I was gonna be coming over to your house with Eli on Friday for the back-to-school party you were having."

"I remember that now." People around Bethany had been laughing, but I thought someone must have told a joke. Not one at her expense. I'd just been welcoming Bethany to high school.

"After that, everyone realized who I was," she said, arching a brow. "Eli's little sister. So they backed off and left me alone." She shrugged. "Even back then, you were always nice to me."

I smiled, and we kept working.

Maybe I had unknowingly rescued her that day, but more than anything, I had thought it was a good excuse to spend time with her. My motives hadn't been 100% pure.

Back then, I'd always been able to keep it in check. Now, I wasn't sure I could keep my feelings under wraps.

But I also refused to do Eli like that. I had to be honest with him before giving in to how I felt about Bethany.

Was it possible he could understand? Maybe even come to accept it?

I had no idea, but I had to try.

13

BETHANY

I was glad when I saw Kane packing snowballs at the park near Cider Center because my mind had been spinning since our almost-kiss in the auditorium.

At first, I had felt disappointed that we'd been interrupted by my mom's phone call. *Finally* having a chance to see what kissing Kane felt like.

Then, embarrassment had taken over because he was my brother's best friend, after all. What would Eli think if he knew I'd kissed Kane? I mean, how were you supposed to navigate that? Especially when Kane had made a promise to Eli to check on me? Eli clearly didn't think Kane and I were romantically interested in each other.

But, today, when Kane acted all nervous at the sight of me, it clicked into place...

Kane had almost kissed me.

All this time, I thought he was indifferent to me, at best. Felt sorry for me, at worst. But you didn't kiss a girl unless you liked her. Kane *must* have feelings for me.

But he held back when we were packing snow-balls, never getting closer than two feet from me. Something was holding him back.

I had walked two blocks past the sewing club before I'd realized I'd done so.

My feet skidded on the icy sidewalk as I stopped in my tracks, cheeks blazing hot even though no one was around to see me. Tucking a strand of curly red hair behind my ear, I reminded myself that I needed to stay focused if I was going to do this fashion show and my application justice.

Finishing my mental pep talk, I turned around and went back to the sewing club room where the ladies were already abuzz and working on plans for the fashion show. Mrs. Katz was planning makeup for each of the looks and showed me her plans on a sketchpad similar to my book of designs.

I told her how much I loved it before Mrs. Cole caught my attention.

She wanted to have candy bars for guests matching the colors of my designs. "Wow," I said, looking at the list of treats she was planning. "It's really coming together."

She smiled. "I'm glad you like it."

Grandma had come early, making calls to local handymen to build the catwalk from the stage. After saying hi to everyone, I got my sewing stuff out to get to work on the main piece of the collection. It was a dress I'd be wearing for the fashion show, and it would be the grand finale.

Even if I did have doubts about my ability to pull off such a fancy dress.

I let out a big breath and told myself to worry about that later. I needed to finish the dress before stressing about how it would look on me.

By the end of our usual sewing club time, I had made good progress on my dress, even if it wasn't quite where it needed to be.

"Hello, hello!" A voice chirped from the front door. It was Starla, Mrs. Katz's assistant. She held a big stack of flyers in her hands as she approached Mrs. Katz. She set the foot-tall pile heavily on the table next to her boss's sketch pad.

Mrs. Katz grinned and said, "Bethany, you have to see these flyers Starla designed."

"I hadn't even thought of flyers," I admitted as I set my dress down and approached the table.

"That's what you have us for," Starla said, passing me a sheet.

My mouth practically fell open. They looked fantastic. I looked up at her. "You designed these?" I asked. As she nodded, I added, "Thank you so much."

The flyers were red, white, and green to match the colors of my designs. They had all the important information, but best of all, had the cutest tagline: SLAY THE SEASON AT EVERY SIZE.

Grandma came up to us then and looked approvingly at the flyers. "These will be perfect. We'll need all the people there we can get."

It wasn't long before Starla had to get back to the salon. I thanked her again before she went. The members of the sewing club quickly divided up the flyers and decided who would be hanging up or passing out flyers where.

Seeing them all with flyers in their hands all of a sudden made the fashion show feel more real than ever. Gratitude overwhelmed me. These ladies had helped me improve my sewing, encouraged me to apply for this program, and now they were doing everything they could to help me get in. I could never thank them enough.

When they were all gone, I sat back down at my table but found it hard to concentrate. I was feeling more and more nervous now that they were publicizing the show. What would all the people in town think? Would they come at all? And if they did, what would happen if I didn't finish everything in time?

Usually when I doubted myself, I got together with my friends, but I hadn't seen them in what felt like ages. They were all busy with Christmas activities of their own.

I got my phone out and sent a quick message in our group chat.

Bethany: Hope you're all doing well! I miss you guys. So much to tell you at the New Year's Eve party. But I'd love it if you'd come to my fashion show.

I snapped a pic of the flyer and sent it as well.

With a sigh, I started packing my stuff up, thinking I needed a change in scenery. After a ten-minute walk, and a stop by Stuffer's to grab my favorite cookies, I made it back home and got right back to work on my dress, determined to stay focused.

The cookies and Christmas music playing in the background was helping.

About an hour in, my phone dinged with a text. I thought maybe it was one of my friends responding to my message from earlier, but instead, it was Kane.

Kane: How's it going? Want to make sure I keep my promise to your brother.

I sent him a quick response back letting him know I was fine.

He texted after that, but I didn't even glance at my phone. Instead, I kept my eyes trained on my sewing machine, letting the sound of it drown out my thoughts.

That's another thing I really liked about sewing.

It helped push back the stressful thoughts.

Thoughts like: I wish Kane would text me just because he wanted to, not because he had to.

14

KANE

*T*he next day, I came close to breaking my all-time record for snowball sales.

There were more tourists in Garland for Christmas than ever before. And they were buying lots and lots of snowballs. So many that I sold out a couple hours earlier than usual.

I thought of going home, but I also wanted to see how Bethany was doing. I hadn't heard from her since the day before when I'd texted her. Maybe I would go see her. See if there was anything she needed for the fashion show.

It was the perfect excuse to see her.

But I wouldn't show up empty handed. I walked across the street to Cocoa Corner and ordered two large cocoas to go, with extra marshmallows. I knew Bethany loved marsh-mallows.

By the time I made it to her grandmother's house, they would surely be the perfect melty consistency. I smiled to myself thinking how she'd smile after the first sip. She always did that with hot cocoa.

When I got to her grandma's house, Mrs. Hart let me in saying Bethany was busy working in her room.

"Thank you," I told her, and I made my way down the hallway, hot chocolates still in hand.

Bethany's door was halfway open. Her sewing machine whirred loudly, and when I reached the doorway, I saw her hunched over it, her fingers delicately and slowly pushing fabric through the machine. It looked like that kind of stuff that ballerina skirts were made out of. Big and fluffy and light.

From this angle, I had a clear view of her profile, and I couldn't help but notice how cute she looked when she was deep in concentration.

A second later, she finally noticed me and jumped, making a loud squeaking noise. The sound of the sewing machine came to a stop. "Oh my gosh, Kane, I didn't see you come in."

Feeling guilty, I quickly apologized. "Sorry, I didn't want to interrupt you. Is it okay?" I gestured at the dress with my hands.

She gave it a closer look, nodding.

"Good." I smiled and handed her one of the hot chocolates. The one I hadn't been sipping from.

I noticed how she sort of avoided my eyes as she took the hot chocolate. When her hand brushed mine, I could've sworn she gave a small gasp. "I thought maybe you could use a little break," I said.

Bethany took a small sip of the hot chocolate and smiled just like I'd hoped. "Hm, this is really good." She set her hot chocolate down carefully on her desk. "But I can't." She glanced at me. "Take a break, I mean."

I nodded toward the dress still in the sewing machine. "How's it going?"

"Good," she said, moving over so I could really see the dress. "This is the main piece. It's really coming along, but I still have a lot of work to do."

The way she wouldn't really meet my eyes made me wonder if I'd messed up with more than just Eli. Maybe *she* didn't want to be more than friends either.

"It's a beautiful dress," I said, looking at the material.

"Thank you." She set her cocoa aside and fiddled with a setting on the sewing machine. But now that my attention was drawn to her instead of the dress, she seemed stressed. There were darker circles under her eyes like she'd had trouble sleeping lately–or maybe she'd just been up late at night working on her application.

"Come on, Bethany," I told her, taking a step closer. "When's the last time you got some fresh air?"

Her gaze was still on the sewing machine. "Yesterday."

"Hm-hm," I said in response. "I bet some fresh air will do you good, help keep the creative juices flowing or whatever."

She sighed, sitting back in er chair. "I guess you're right." She got up and stretched her arms. "My back could use a break." She turned to me. "So what did you have in mind?"

I grinned. "How about a ride on Rudolph's sleigh?"

That made her crack a smile. Finally. "Are we ten?" she teased. "I haven't ridden the sleigh in years."

I shrugged. "You can never be too old for a good ole ride on Rudolph's sleigh."

We went outside, hot chocolate in hand, and found Rudolph's sleigh down the road, waiting for another round of passengers.

I began jogging. "Come on!"

When we got there, I held the door open for Bethany, who climbed in first while holding my other hand.

"Thanks," she said.

"Of course." I climbed in after her, and Rudolph snapped the reins making the horses take off.

We went down a hill fast, and Bethany shrieked. Without thinking much about it, I held her hand. When we slowed back down, I let go.

She didn't mention the hand-holding, but she did grin over at me. "You're right, I needed this," she said.

My lips lifted to match her smile. "I know I've probably been sort of a bother the last few days, but seeing your dedication to the fashion show has been amazing."

As she looked at the Christmas lights around us, she shook her head. "It's no big deal."

But she shouldn't downplay her effort. "I've

seen athletes who don't work as hard as you, Bethany. You should really be proud of yourself."

That's when her gentle smile began to fade. "I just hate to think it won't be enough, you know?" She looked at me now, dark eyes reflecting the lights behind me. Curls slipped from her braid, wild around her face.

I tucked her hair behind her ear. The same strand of red hair that always got in her way. "If anyone can do this, it's you. And I'll be here if you need anything."

It was just us in the back of the sleigh, and I realized how close she was to me.

Her green eyes met mine. "Because of my brother?" she asked. There was a hint of sadness to the question.

I wanted to give her an honest answer to that but couldn't.

And it was just as well because our magical sleigh ride had come to an end. We were back near her house.

The small sleigh door opened, and Rudolph stood there and helped us out. I paid and thanked him.

"I guess I'll see you tomorrow?" I asked Bethany once the sleigh was gone. It was Christmas Eve, and her parents were getting back Christmas day. The fashion show was the following day.

Bethany nodded. "If you want to. We're having a dress rehearsal before the show."

After giving me the rehearsal time, she waved and turned towards her grandmother's house.

I stood there, watching her go and deciding to finally talk to her brother.

On Christmas Eve, I got to the school early for the dress rehearsal. I had to make sure I had plenty of time to get everything ready.

Hot chocolate in hand, I walked backstage and began getting all of the outfits lined up for the models. They were finally done aside from alterations I'd need to make for the models. With all the hangers lined up and perfectly spaced, I let out a shaky exhale. The closer we got to the show, the more nervous I got.

Not only would half the town be at the fashion show, thanks to the flyers placed in every window and taped to every light pole, but my parents and brother would also be back in time to take their place in the front row.

They were going to see everything I had been working so hard for.

So would Kane.

I kept telling myself there was no reason for things to be weird between him and me. Or between Eli and me. Nothing had happened. Nothing would happen. Even if my feelings for him were more real than ever.

Time seemed to move in hyper speed as the dress rehearsal began. All the models arrived—mainly college students who were home over break—and started getting ready. We had water ready for them and snacks too. Thankfully, Scrooge had offered to donate food for the models after the show. One thing about Scrooge, he pretended to be a Grinch, and he was, but deep, deep, deep down inside, he had a heart of gold.

The models each tried on their outfits, and I went one by one, making last-minute adjustments and suggestions on how to pose to best showcase the designs.

Luckily, they were naturals. And by the time they finished strutting the stage, their excitement had infected me too. The sewing club ladies weren't just expert seamstresses–they had brought all the details together perfectly.

This was really happening. In less than forty-eight hours, the fashion show would be underway.

And so would my application to the fashion program with my dresses and a video of the event.

While everyone started packing up to go home, I stood near the velvety red curtains and glanced around at the stage and the rows of seats.

None of it would've been possible without this perfect location, which wouldn't have been possible without Kane.

I really owed him.

A loud sound of tape being pulled from the roll jarred me from my thoughts, and I followed the sound to see Kane taping down a cord behind one of the lit up stars. As if he felt me watching him, he met my gaze and grinned.

One by one, everyone left until it was just Kane and me. "You can head home," I told him. "I just have a few last things to do.

He let his hands fall to his sides. "Tell me what to do. I'm yours."

My stomach did somersaults at the sound of those words, and I tried not to think about it too much.

Despite the butterflies in my stomach begging for my attention, I explained how the snowflakes weren't quite right from the back row, and we got to touching up the paint to add more silver that would catch the lights better. Then I began cutting up some sparkly felt snowflakes to add to the dark red stage curtains. They would look magical under the bright lights.

By the time we were finally done, it was late, and I was tired but wired. Still, we had to finish cleaning up so it wouldn't be a mess for the show.

We headed back to the costume room with the leftover paint and other supplies.

"You ready to break a leg soon?" Kane asked with a kind smile.

I exhaled. "I sure hope so."

We began putting stuff away, and Kane said, "What do you mean you hope?" He turned to me, hands now empty. "You've put in all the hard work." Waving his hands in the direction of the stage. "You turned your vision into a reality, Bethany." Then he took a few steps toward me until he was just a few inches away. "This is your moment, and you made it happen."

My brain failed to come up with a response, overwhelmed with my own emotions. He was right. I'd put in all the work. And he'd helped me more than he ever needed to make good on his promise with my brother.

Kane took my hand, and his eyes locked on mine. "I'll believe in you enough for both of us until you believe in you."

I couldn't believe how close he was. "Because you're my brother's best friend?" I managed. I wanted it to be more than that.

If something was about to happen between us, I had to hear it from his mouth first. Hear how he actually felt about me.

"No," he said quietly. "Because I'm falling for you."

Then, before I could really think about whether we should or not, he was closing the distance between us and his mouth was on mine.

My arms went around his neck like I'd done it a hundred times before, and his hands settled around my waist.

All my wishes from Christmases past must have been waiting for this moment, because Kane's kiss was better than I'd ever imagined.

16

KANE

$\mathcal{I}$ woke up on cloud nine the next morning. All day, I felt like I was floating from place to place. And I knew I probably had the cheesiest grin on my face, too.

The kiss last night with Bethany... I couldn't get her off my mind.

But that wasn't all that was on my mind.

I had tried to call Eli the night before, but he'd texted me and said we'd catch up when he was home.

Eli would be back in town later today, and I knew I needed to talk to him. It was only right I tell him the truth. I would never want him to think I was keeping something like this from him on purpose. The betrayal could really hurt our friendship. Especially if he found out about our kiss from Bethany.

I could ask her to keep it between us, but that's not how I wanted to do things. If this was going to work out with Bethany—and I had every intention of it working out perfectly with her—then I needed to talk to him before he got back to town.

So during the hour I was closed for lunch, I pulled out my phone and dialed his number.

Thankfully, he picked up right away.

"Hey, man! I'm glad you called," he said. I could hear the noise of an airport in the background, and his voice was loud and full of excitement.

I greeted him back, and he dove straight into telling me everything about his college tour.

"I think this is it, Kane," he said. "I really do. The campus is great. The baseball program here is awesome. I like the coaches. I'm pretty sure this is where I'm going to end up next year. I mean, I can really see myself here, you know?"

I grinned to myself. "That's great, man. I'm glad to hear such good news." Even though a twinge of sadness hit that we'd likely be at different colleges.

"But anyway," Eli said, "enough about me. How have you been doing? How's Bethany? I haven't been able to talk to her really. I just hear she's been super busy with a fashion show?" he asked.

I cleared my throat. "Yeah, actually, that's what I wanted to talk to you about."

"About the fashion show?" He sounded confused.

I glanced down, pushing aside some snow with my boot. "About Bethany," I managed.

"Bethany? Is she okay?" Eli asked. He'd been so excited earlier, but now he seemed worried.

"Yeah, she's great. It's not that. It's actually... Well, I would never want you to think I was hiding anything from you, but... I really like her. You know, like..."

"Oh," I heard Eli say on the other end of the phone. The only noise was someone on the airport loudspeaker announcing a gate change.

When the announcement ended, I said, "I know I'm not supposed to like your sister, and if you just say the word, I'll put an end to things right now."

I heard him exhale. "Put an end to things, huh?"

There was a beat or two where neither of us said anything.

Then Eli said, "So what changed?"

I rolled my lips together. He was my best friend–

we talked about everything and anything. But it was hard to talk with him about his sister. Still, I wanted to be honest with him. "Nothing changed, really. I guess I've liked her for a long time, but I always thought it would be wrong to really pursue her like that. Our friendship was too important."

"And it's not important now?" he asked.

I bit my lip. "Of course it is."

He sighed. "I am glad you're telling me about it and not sneaking around…"

My stomach dipped with guilt for not telling him before now. "But?"

That's when he chuckled a little bit, and I finally breathed in relief. "Okay, man," I heard Eli finally say. "Okay, I trust you. It's alright with me as long as you promise to treat her right. I would never want our friendship to suffer, because I'd have to choose my sister."

It stung a little to hear him say those words, but I totally understood where he was coming from. I would've said the same exact thing about my little brother.

"I completely understand," I told him.

"Good," he said. "Then I'm glad that's out of the way."

We hung up not long after that, and I breathed a huge sigh of relief.

I was glad I had gotten that off my chest. And Eli had taken it way better than I expected. But still, it all just felt kind of… odd that this now had a real shot at becoming something real. Bethany and I would have a chance at being more than friends, after all these years.

I would get to call her mine. Walk hand in hand with her.

Kiss her again and again without feeling guilty.

I was over the moon about it, and I couldn't wait to tell her. Maybe after the fashion show, though, so she could really focus on it. She was almost at the finish line. I didn't want to distract her from something so important. Tomorrow had to go perfectly.

17

BETHANY

*T*he day after Christmas, I left the house early to go to the school and prepare for the show, carrying the final piece of my collection in a garment bag. It was a gorgeous green ballgown with a flowing skirt and lace sleeves.

As my feet crunched fresh snow on the sidewalk, I thought of what it would be like to wear it on the runway. I'd stayed up all night to perfect the dress, but I still felt nervous to wear it in front of so many people, including my family and Kane.

Fate must have heard me thinking of him, because as I turned the corner, I nearly ran into him.

"Kane!" I cried out in surprise. "I almost hit you."

He gave me a sheepish grin. "Thought I'd come early and see if any work needed to be done." He rubbed his hand over my shoulder, making electricity spark through my plum-colored coat. "Guess I wasn't early enough."

My lips tipped up as I said, "Great minds think alike."

He took the garment bag from me, easily carrying it in one of his large hands, and then slipped his other hand into mine. My brain nearly short-circuited. *Kane was holding my hand!* Neither of us had gloves on, and his skin was so warm on mine against the chilly air.

"My brother said you talked to him yesterday," I said. My cheeks still felt hot remembering that conversation.

His lips formed a small smile. "Sorry, I should have warned you. I was just glad he gave me permission to pursue things with you."

The thrum of my heart grew even faster at that sentence. "He did?"

Kane nodded. "Looking back, I should have warned you... What did he say to you?"

I tipped my head to the side. "Well... A lot."

He cringed. "Oh no."

I shook my head, walking slowly toward the

school just to keep his hand in mine a little longer before we had to get to work. "He wrote out a list of ground rules for us to follow if we decide to start dating so I could get his 'blessing.'"

Kane's dark eyebrows shot up. "What's it say?"

The folded piece of notebook paper was still in my pocket, so I let go of Kane's hand to get it and open it up. We both stalled on the sidewalk, looking at Eli's neat writing. He must have been in a mood because the pen indentations were deep in the page.

1. No PDA. None. Nada. Zilch.
2. You AND Kane still have to prioritize your friends. No blowing everyone else off all the time to be with each other.
3. If you break up, try be on good terms. I don't want to choose between my friend and my sister. (I'll choose you, just so you know. But please don't make me.)

Kane's eyes darted back and forth across the page, until he got to the end and gave me a small smile. "I think we can manage that."

My smile grew—gosh my cheeks were going to

have super strength from all this smiling I was doing lately!

Folding up the letter, I said, "We should probably get started."

He nodded, walking alongside me to the heavy metal door that led to the backstage area of the theater. Before I could reach the handle, he grabbed it and held the door open for me. I thanked him as I went inside, but the words died in my throat.

Kane turned on the lights. The door slammed shut behind us.

I couldn't believe what we were looking at. My jaw fell open, my throat felt tight, and I was sure I'd collapse at any moment with how weak my legs felt.

"Oh my gosh," I heard myself say.

Kane stood beside me. "What could have happened to cause all of this?"

The costume room with the rack full of my designs was in *shambles*. Torn pieces of clothing covered the floor along with pens and pencils and pretty much everything else that had previously been on a table.

Bending over, I picked up a design to see if it was salvageable. But there were shreds in the fabric, and it damp and muddy too. Even if I could fix the tears, the stains were yet another problem.

My stomach turned as we walked over to the rack, stepping over the cluttered floor.

There was just one design left hanging, a matching set with pleated pants and a loose sweater. Even though it was just barely dangling on the hanger, it was still intact. Everything else? It was in pieces all around me.

How could this be possible?

Kane went back to the door and checked the latch, inside and out.

I stared at him, thinking back to last night. We'd been the last ones out. "We forgot to lock the door behind us, didn't we?" I managed, my voice catching in my throat.

"Bethany," he said, holding the door open but turning to look at me. "I'm sorry. I'm really sorry."

I bent down to pick up what had been a beautiful holiday dress but was now just a torn piece of blue fabric. I let it fall to the ground again. "It's all gone."

I stood up, eyes watering. "The fashion show… I'll have to cancel it."

Kane let the door close again and he walked

over to me. "There's gotta be something we can do. You can just—"

I held my hand up, not letting him get close to me. "There's nothing we can do!" I shouted. My chest rose up and down quickly with how hard I was breathing. "Everything's ruined."

Tears filled my eyes as I took it all in around me. The truth sank in forming a weight on my chest so heavy I thought I'd never really be able to fully breathe again. Not only was the fashion show cancelled, I wouldn't have near enough time to re-create these designs in time for the application deadline. Definitely not at the same level of quality.

Taking the garment bag from Kane, I carefully hung it up on the now-empty rack. The zipper was loud in the silent room as I slid it down. Once it was open, my fingers lightly grazed the finished dress. This and a matching set was all that I had to show for my months of hard work and saving for the best fabrics.

I zipped up the garment bag again. It wouldn't be enough to meet the minimum requirements, much less help me earn a spot in the fashion program.

A single tear rolled down my cheek, and I

wiped it away.

It was over.

Just like that, it was all over.

Kane came up to me and put his hand on my shoulder. "We can fix this, Bethany," he said quietly. "Maybe some of the pieces will just need minor repairs."

I shrugged his hand off. "There's no fixing this," I said. I knew my voice was harsh, but I couldn't find it in me to care.

I let the anger take a hold of me, because if I didn't and I let the tears keep flowing, I knew I'd never stop crying. And I didn't want to cry, not here, not now in front of Kane.

I wiped at my eyes and then picked up garment bag and the matching set. "This was my fault for letting myself get distracted with you."

Hurt flashed through Kane's eyes. I immediately felt guilty, but I kept going because I couldn't hold all this pain inside. "If I hadn't let myself get distracted, then I would've made sure to lock the door last night. Whatever animal did this wouldn't have been able to get in. It's all my fault."

My mouth contorted as I fought the urge to break down into sobs.

"Bethany, you're hurting right now, you–" Kane began, but I didn't let him finish.

"I am hurting right now," I confirmed. "But I can also finally see the truth." I took a step back from him. "I've liked you so much all of these years, but you were never interested until now. I should've taken the hint and fully devoted myself to my dreams, not pining for you endlessly," I spat out.

Even with all those mean words, Kane came toward me and tried to console me. Now the tears were really coming on, and it was all I could do to not completely break down in front of him. If he hugged me, I'd completely fall apart.

So I turned away from him and ran.

All of the beautiful moments we'd shared recently?

The kiss last night?

It all felt tainted now.

I hurried down the sidewalk wishing I could already be home.

My dreams? They were over now. For good.

*S*tanding alone in that mess of a dressing room, I felt shell-shocked.

It was like a bomb had gone off here, blowing up Bethany's designs, her dreams, and even the start of our relationship.

I was absolutely crushed for her. Her entire fashion show... gone, just like that.

And I felt guilty for whatever part I may have played in the designs getting torn up. Coach *had* said the door was tricky. But how were we supposed to know it would lead to something like this?

My chest still ached from the force of Bethany's words. She'd hurled them at me just as harshly as she'd blamed herself. I couldn't help but feel betrayed after everything I had done for her. All the time I'd spent helping her out when I could have been working at my kiosk or creating new posts to advertise it on social media.

Bethany didn't owe me a thing–I'd done it all gladly. I just couldn't believe she tossed me aside so quickly.

I couldn't leave the dressing room like this, her designs shredded and all over the floor, so I started cleaning up. I hung up what I could and carefully folded the rest, still hoping she might be able to repair the outfits or use the fabric scraps to make something new.

But with everything picked up, there was nothing more for me to do here. I made my way home, eyes downcast, shoulders slumped, and still hearing her words ringing in my ears.

Just when I thought Bethany and I might finally have a chance, everything had blown up in our faces in a split second.

A couple of people said hi to me on the way home, even asked how I was doing, but I didn't have the heart to do much but wave hello and say, "I'm fine, thank you for asking."

I walked around for a while, not wanting to go home.

But then it got colder and the sky turned gray, and I decided it wasn't doing me much good to freeze my nose off.

When I got home, my parents were already getting lunch ready. As I took off my gear, I could hear the music from the kitchen. Their favorite thing to do was cook together, and they even got all lovey-dovey about it.

Usually, it made me cringe a little. I was glad they genuinely loved each other, but they were my mom and dad. I didn't need to see all that.

But today, it just felt sad watching them happy together. It felt like I'd never have a real chance at something like that with Bethany.

So when I got home, I let them know I was heading upstairs and that I wasn't very hungry.

"But we're making your favorite," my mom called after me. "Hot chili!"

I continued trudging down the hall to my room. "Maybe later," I told them, not even bothering to turn back. In the safety of my room, I closed the door behind me and let myself fall on the bed.

How had my life blown up in just one morning? It had to be a new record.

Guy likes girl for years.

Guy finally gets girl.

Guy immediately loses girl.

And now...

Girl hates guy.

I groaned into my pillow.

That talk with Eli, not to mention putting our friendship at risk, all of it had been for nothing.

I didn't even want to think about how awkward it would be around Eli and Bethany now. Going to their house... it would never be the same. Not if she hated my guts and felt like I took away her dreams.

I rolled over until I was on my back and stared at the ceiling. A big sigh escaped my chest. This was hopeless.

A little scratching sound caught my attention. I sat up and looked at Jason, my pet hedgehog. I stood up and walked over to his cage, carefully picking him up.

He tucked his head and chest into himself until he was a small, prickly ball. I took a seat at my desk, holding him close to my chest. After a moment, he uncurled and climbed up to my shoulder.

My smile shook a bit as I watched him. He

could always cheer me up, even on the gloomiest of days, but there was a first time for everything.

Not even Jason was going to mend my broken heart. Not today, anyway.

After a few minutes of letting him scurry around my desk, I picked him back up and put him back in his cage.

When I looked out my window, the sky was a dull gray and fresh snow was falling down.

Usually, on a day off, I would stay up and game or something, but I wasn't in the mood right now. So even though it was still early, I got ready for bed and turned out the light.

Maybe, just maybe, tomorrow would be a better day.

19
BETHANY

I hugged the pillow closer to me, wishing I could just sleep and get a reprieve from thinking about everything that had happened.

But no matter how hard I squeezed my eyes together, I couldn't fall asleep.

Tears ran down my cheeks–had been coming ever since I got out of Kane's sight–but I didn't bother to wipe them away. I couldn't remember the last time I'd cried this hard about anything.

That was because nothing in my life had ever been as important as getting into this fashion program.

Now, no matter how I looked at the situation, my dreams of getting into the fashion program were gone. Which meant my chance of becoming a big-name fashion designer was getting smaller.

The sewing club ladies had been wrong to believe in me. Thinking of them made my face turn hot with embarrassment. They had taken so much time to help me with both my designs and the fashion show, and it had all been for nothing. How could I ever face them again? I felt humiliated, especially knowing flyers about my fashion show had been posted all over town.

All because I let myself get distracted by Kane's kiss and didn't make sure the door to the school was locked. I'd crushed on him forever, and the minute he had expressed that maybe he felt the same about me, I'd let that get completely in the way of reaching my own dreams.

How could I have been so careless?

Boys would always be there.

An opportunity like this wouldn't.

When the door to my room opened with a creak, I let out a heavy sigh and sat up, rubbing my eyes. I wasn't ready to talk about it yet, although I knew I'd need to sooner or later.

"What's wrong?" Eli asked. "Shouldn't you be leaving soon?"

He was never one to get sappy with me, but he could probably guess I wasn't my normal self.

I shrugged. "The fashion show kind of got ruined." My voice cracked on the words.

"Ruined?" he asked, brow furrowed.

I told him everything. How I was planning to stand out with the fashion show and submit the video as the main part of my application. The mess we'd found in the theater earlier. I even fessed up and told him how rude I'd been to Kane.

That made his brows pinch, but he said, "And you don't know what could've caused everything to be destroyed?"

I shook my head. "I don't know. It looked like some kind of animal got in—although I guess it doesn't really matter at this point, does it?"

Eli just sat there, staring at the wall in front of him as he took it all in. "There's gotta be a way to fix it," he said finally. "And I'm sure Kane will understand. It had to have been a shock."

"I don't think so," I said, pretty sure I'd messed it all up for good.

He patted my knee. "Let me know if there's anything I can do?"

I nodded, and he left, still sporting a concerned look.

The idea of him leaving next year probably had him feeling some sort of way because Eli never was this kind to me, but it was nice.

My phone rang with a number I didn't recognize. Since it looked local, I went ahead and answered it.

"Hello?" I said, holding the phone up to my ear.

"Hello? Is this Bethany? This is Coach Michaels." He was the baseball coach–the one Kane had asked a favor of. He said he was calling to apologize about the door and everything that had happened. Kane told him about it.

"That door latch never did work properly," he said with a guilty tone to his voice. "We should've gotten it fixed a long time ago. When I checked the cameras, I couldn't believe the size of the bear that found its way in. Really, you guys are lucky you weren't there when it happened. We don't usually see them much this time of year, but they're always looking for food."

I thought of all the snacks I'd left out for the models in preparation for the show.

"Listen, I just want you to know I'm sorry about what happened. It wasn't your fault," he said.

My throat tightened up and a fresh round of tears wet my stinging eyes. "It wasn't?"

"Not at all. You could have locked it, and that bear still might have gotten in. I'm so sorry, Bethany."

I thanked him for calling me, and we hung up.

Numb, I lay back on my bed, taking in the news.

That door latch hadn't been working properly anyway. It wouldn't have mattered whether I had remembered to lock the door behind me or not. Maybe we had.

Which made me feel even worse about all of the hurtful words I had said to Kane. I had ruined that too.

My parents told me I wasn't allowed to stay in my room and mope, so I decided I might as well open up the snowball shop. I was hard at work making snowballs when I heard the sound of footsteps in the snow behind me.

I turned around to find Eli walking up my driveway, his breath lifting in small puffs of fog.

"Hey, man," he called out with a wave.

I stood up and waved back. "Hey." I tried to smile. Maybe it worked because he grinned back at me.

"I'm back," he said. His smile made my shoulders relax at least a little bit. He wouldn't be smiling at me if he hated my guts. But all that relief went away when I realized it was entirely possible he didn't know what had happened yet.

My parents had a couple chairs on the front porch that the overhang protected from snow, so I got up from my knees and waved him over to join me. It was time for a break anyway. I wiped the sweat from my brow, waiting to see how this conversation would go.

"I heard, man," Eli said finally, and I let out a big exhale.

I turned to him, speaking quickly. "I'm sorry, man. I didn't expect things with Bethany to just blow up in my face like that. I wouldn't have come to you other—"

He held up a hand. "I don't blame you," he said, looking around. "And I don't blame Bethany either. I guess things just happen."

"Yeah," I replied, looking down at my blue snow boots. My chest felt tight, and I had to blink back the stinging in my eyes. "I do hope Bethany's doing okay, and that it all works out for her, even if I'm bummed it didn't work out for us." I exhaled. There was something else I had to get off my chest. "I'm sorry if I let you down, man."

Eli didn't say anything for a minute, and I wondered if it was because he really was upset with me. Would our friendship ever be the same now?

Softly, Eli said, "I'm not disappointed with you."

I looked at him, not sure what to say next.

He leaned forward, his eyes serious, one brow up like when he had something important to say to the baseball team before a game. "Listen, I get that all of this sucks, Kane, but what I'm really wondering is why you aren't doing anything about it."

My own brow furrowed in confusion. "What do you mean?" I asked.

"I mean," he said, a little louder this time. "What are you going to do about it?"

I stood up and shook my head. Even since we were kids, Eli and I were never ones to argue or fight. Never. But this felt different. "This isn't a baseball game, man. It's not the bottom of the ninth with the team down by two. There's nothing to be done. The game is over."

Eli stood up too, the corner of his mouth turned up in a sly smile. "Oh, the game is far from over, my friend."

"I hate it when you go into baseball captain mode," I responded lamely.

That made his grin grow wider.

"You know I'm right," he replied.

I shook my head again. "If Bethany says things are done, then I'm going to respect that." I paused, the last words she said to me ringing through my ears clearly again. She blamed me, at least partially, for everything that happened. "Besides, she said things." I hesitated to say more. "She made me see that I've been a distraction to her." I took a beat. "It wasn't right of me to try and push my feelings on her." I'd never want to be the person standing in the way of her dreams. Fashion mattered so much to her.

Eli walked over until he was toe to toe with me. I could tell he was determined to talk me out of what I had already decided was best for everyone all around.

"Stop giving me that look," I said, standing my ground. "I'm staying out of her way, and that's that."

"'That's that,' huh?" he said feigning nonchalance.

I glared at him, wishing my best friend wasn't so freaking stubborn.

"Look, when Bethany's mad, she tells me that my breath smells worse than a donkey's butt and that no girl would ever want to kiss me, but where would I be if I believed every word she said, huh?" He winked.

I shoved his shoulder, fighting back a laugh. "What's your point?"

"The point is people say things in the heat of the moment sometimes, things that they don't really mean, but you can't let it ruin everything," he went on. "You can't let this ruin whatever chance you two had."

I stared at him, not believing he was fighting so hard for this to work out.

"Don't give me that look," he said. "You'd have to be blind to not notice how crazy you two are about each other. I knew this was coming sooner or later, and honestly, I'm surprised it took you two this long." He playfully shoved my shoulder back.

We were quiet for a moment. Eli sat back down, and then I did too.

"So?" Eli asked finally. "I know you care about her too much to let her cry in her bed for the rest of break."

I looked at him. "You're right," I began. "I have an idea. But I'm going to need your help."

BETHANY

$\mathcal{I}$t had been a couple days since everything had gone down with Kane, and even though I'd tried all my usual tricks, I still didn't feel better.

Watching America's Next Top Model re-runs didn't help, neither did Say Yes to the Dress or Project Runway. It reminded me that I'd missed my chance at this application window. I'd have to wait another year to apply, which meant I'd also have to create new designs to be fashion-forward, save more money for materials. And I'd be busy with my senior year and college applications.

I tried going for a walk, but I avoided half of town because I didn't want to run into Kane by accident. I was so ashamed of how I treated him.

To make matters worse, I didn't have my friends around to vent to and cry with. They would understand how devastating this was. But I also knew they were all busy making things happen for themselves, and I didn't have the heart to rain on their parades. I'd tell them all about it at Haley's New Year's party.

Maybe then the pain wouldn't be so bad.

My family could tell I was hurting too. After Eli talked to me, so did my mom and then my dad. When Grandma came into my room, I doubted even she could make me feel better.

She took a seat at the end of my bed. "It's sewing club today," she tried. "I'd love you to come with me."

I gave her what I was sure was a lame smile while the constant ache in my chest intensified. "Not today, Grandma. I can't face them yet," I said.

She exhaled and patted my leg. "We understand how devastated you must be after everything."

I wasn't sure they totally understood, but I appreciate the sentiment all the same.

"The ladies at sewing club were just as devastated," she went on. "We all worked so hard to make that fashion show happen, just for that bear to get in. It's a shame."

"Can you let them know how much I appreciate all their hard work? And how sorry I am that it was all for nothing?" I said quietly. My voice was shaky with grief.

She pressed her mouth into a thin line. "Maybe you could tell them yourself?" she tried again. "It could be good for you to be around people who love you."

My eyes welled up with tears again at the thought of showing my face at sewing club. "I can't," I told her, my voice breaking.

She patted my leg some more. "There, there. I won't make you go."

"I just need a break from… everything," I said.

She nodded. "You know, I get the feeling there's a lot more bothering you than just the fashion show, even if it is a big deal in and of itself."

I looked away, not wanting to admit my heart was breaking for more reason than one. I could have shared the burden of my disappointment with Kane, but I'd pushed him away. Guilt made me feel like I deserved to be alone right now.

"How's Kane? Have you talked to him?" she asked like she could sense me thinking about him.

I shook my head. Part of me wanted to tell her what had happened with him, but just like the fashion show, I was embarrassed and devastated.

"Are things alright with him?" Grandma pressed.

I shook my head again, fighting back tears.

"Oh, Bethany," she replied. "What happened with you two?"

My lips trembled, and a tear slid down my cheek.

She gave me a small, sad smile. "I always knew you two would end up together. That boy always liked you, I could tell. And I could tell you liked him just as much."

I couldn't help but sniffle. A tear ran down my cheek at the thought of everything that had happened between us in the last week—and how fast it had all come crumbling down. "It was just a dumb winter fling," I said. "Over before it even got started."

"A fling?" Grandma said, almost sounding offended. "Bethany, that boy loves you."

I shrugged. "Well, if that's true, I made sure he'd regret it."

Grandma didn't say anything, so I went on.

"I said a lot of mean things to him that day," I cried, tears falling down my cheeks. "I blamed him for my designs getting ruined, even though it wasn't his fault."

Grandma came closer to me, putting her hand on my shoulder. "Bethany, like the kids say these days, I'm going to 'get real' with you."

I couldn't help but laugh a little hearing her trying to sound hip.

"We all make mistakes and say things we regret. Lord knows I had my fair share of spats with your grandpa while he was alive," she said. "The important thing is to apologize and do better. Never make a mistake without learning from it."

I wiped away the tears. "Okay," I replied.

She leaned down and kissed my forehead. "You're a good person, Bethany. And I know Kane cares for you. He showed you how much he cares, which is even better than him saying it out loud. I know you won't let a mistake stand between the two of you."

After that, she got up and left, shutting my bedroom door silently behind her.

I knew it was impossible to fix my designs in time for the application, but I knew one thing I could fix right now. And I had a feeling it would help me feel better, too.

I had to talk to Kane.

I picked up my phone to text him and ask if he could meet me to talk in person.

But a text from Kane was already waiting for me.

Kane: Can you meet me at the ice-skating rink on the 30th?

I wondered why we wanted to meet, but instead of asking, I just typed a message back.

Bethany: Yes.

After that, I got up from my bed and walked over to my desk.

There was one more thing I had to do.

I opened up my laptop and brought up the webpage that held my application. It was still there, all filled out.

I bit my lip, mourning all of the hard work that I'd put in to make my dream happen.

22

KANE

I'd been too busy to open up the snowball business the last three days.

There was too much to do if I was going to make my idea work. And I was determined to make it work, more than anything else in my life.

So for three days, I hadn't slept or eaten or been home much.

Instead, I'd been running all around Garland talking to people and making things happen.

Luckily, I had quite a few favors I could call in, or my goal would've been impossible.

But now I had a couple more hours until go time, and I was pretty sure I was going to be able to pull it off.

Pretty sure.

At least, that's what I was hoping for.

There were too many things at stake, too many people involved now, for this not to work.

As I walked over the sidewalk sprinkled with salt to keep the ice at by, I grabbed my phone from my pocket and called Mrs. Katz at the sewing club.

"What's the status?" I asked the old woman who owned Vixen's Salon.

"Operation Snow Queen is almost a wrap. Just a few more... loose ends to tie up," she said, and I could tell she was probably grinning at her clever line.

I smiled. "That's fantastic, Mrs. Katz," I said. "I knew I could count on you. Bethany's going to get the surprise of a lifetime."

"Any time," she said. "It's a pleasure doing business with you, Kane."

I had promised to shovel her driveway for the next year in exchange for her help along with the rest of the ladies at sewing club. They had wanted to pitch in and help regardless, but I had insisted on some sort of payment for their time.

I hung up the phone, relieved the most important piece was in place.

Next, I had a stop to make at Fall La La La, the ice-skating rink in town. I had to speak with the manager and make sure everything was set to go.

After that, I would stop at the dry cleaners to pick up something special.

Meanwhile, Eli was talking to the other guys on the baseball team for me.

So far, everything was on track for me to show Bethany that anything was possible in Garland at Christmastime. Hopefully, she'd also see how much she meant to me. I wanted her to see that she could care about me and reach her dreams at the same time; I'd never stand in her way. I wanted to stand by her side.

23

BETHANY

*P*retty soon, I would be meeting up with Kane at the ice-skating rink. I wasn't sure why he wanted to meet there, but it didn't matter to me. I'd meet him in the middle of a snowstorm for a chance to apologize to him. I didn't expect him to forgive me or even like me as a friend after everything I'd said to him, but I hoped it would at least help him feel comfortable hanging out with Eli.

Using a curling iron, I put a few curls in my hair and then threw on some fleece-lined leggings and a Garland High sweater. With my snow boots and beanie on, I threw on a forest-green wool coat and reached for the handle.

"Wait up!" Eli called from behind me.

When I turned to see what he needed, I saw he was carrying my green dress in his arms. The one dress that hadn't been destroyed because I'd been working on it all night for the fashion show.

Just seeing it made my chest ache all over again. "What are you doing?" I managed to ask with a weak voice.

He came up to me, pushing it into my arms. "You should wear it."

I looked from the dress to him, completely puzzled. "I told you. The fashion show... it didn't work out."

He gave me a kind look. "I know, Beth. But I thought you deserved to wear this anyway. Grandma told me how hard you worked on it."

I coughed to clear the sudden frog in my throat. "Um, thanks, but it's not really the right occasion. I could never—"

"Just trust me, okay?" he said softly. There was something in his eyes that had me agreeing.

"But, if I'm gonna wear this, I'm going to need some shoes, huh?" I took the dress and went back to my room to change.

The dress fit like a glove. Plus, the green perfectly contrasted my pale skin and red hair. Since the heels I planned to wear had been ruined at the school, I put on my black platform Converse. Not quite the heels I envisioned, but they would definitely keep the hem from dragging over the sidewalk.

When I walked down the stairs, Eli had his keys in his hands. He smiled at me, gazing at the dress. "It's amazing," he said. "Come on, I'll give you a ride."

I was starting to wonder why Eli was being extra nice to me.

Was he getting sentimental in his senior year?

Or did he just feel sorry for me?

As I shut the car door and buckled in, I said, "Whatever was going on with me and Kane... that's over now. And you don't need to be mad at him. It was my fault. You know that, right?"

"I know," he said with a smile. "I'm not here to pressure you into anything. Like I said, I just thought you should wear that dress tonight is all."

As we pulled up to a stop sign near the rink, Eli turned to me. "I'm really proud of you, you know. No matter what happens."

I tried to smile, but it was hard with him hitting me in my feels. "Senior year sure has you all sentimental," I told him.

That made him laugh. "I guess so. I really am

going to miss you and Kane, though. You two are my two favorite people in the world, and I can't believe I won't be seeing you two every day anymore pretty soon."

"You'll be busy playing at a top school," I told him. "And so will Kane."

He scoffed like it was no big deal, but I could tell he couldn't quite believe his luck. With all the work he'd put into his sport, he deserved to have his dream come true, even if mine had come crashing down.

As he pulled across the intersection, he said, "I just want you to know, if you two ever work it out, you have my blessing, as long as you follow those rules, alright?"

I glanced down at my shoes and didn't say anything. That ship had sailed when I pushed it off a waterfall with my words. Maybe Kane and I could be friends if he forgave me. Even if he ever forgave me, I wasn't sure I could forgive myself.

We finally pulled up to the ice-skating rink, and I got out. "Thank you," I said.

"Good luck." Eli gave me a wave and drove off.

I wondered why he was acting this way. Clearly Kane had told him we were meeting, and I wasn't sure how I felt about my brother knowing so much. Guess that's what happens when you fall for your brother's best friend.

With a steadying breath, I turned to go into the rink. It hadn't snowed all day, but all around me, thick white flakes began falling. I looked up. A half moon hung amongst dark-gray clouds. It was a beautiful night.

As I neared the front window, I noticed a sign out front advertising an event happening tonight.

I wondered what kind of event, and if the rink would be packed. Kane had wanted to talk. Hopefully, it wouldn't be too crowded for us to have a private conversation.

I paid for a ticket and rental skates, even though I might not feel like skating when this was all said and done. Kane was just inside, waiting for me. He rushed over to hold the door open for me.

"Thanks," I said, my cheeks feeling hot. This was the first time I'd seen him since that day, and he was just as handsome as always.

"Bethany," he replied warmly. "I'm glad you came."

Butterflies tickled my stomach, giving me far too much hope. We walked in, and I had no idea what to say to him. "I'm sorry" didn't seem like enough.

He led me to the ice rink, and I saw that nobody was out on the ice, which was odd considering the event.

That's when I noticed the long red carpet laid out on the ice.

There was a large, beautiful lettered sign to my right that said: Charity Fashion Show featuring Hart It Designs by Bethany Hart.

I turned to Kane in utter disbelief. "What's going on?"

24
KANE

I grabbed Bethany's hand and led her to the ice rink, where the red carpet runway began.

She looked absolutely shocked, but there was no time for explanations. I just wanted to show her what I'd been working so hard to make happen for her.

"Wait here," I told Bethany. Mrs. Katz from sewing club had my black blazer ready for me. I pulled it on over my dress shirt and took the microphone from the DJ at the stand nearby.

I walked down the red carpet to the end of the runway by the DJ stand and turned towards Bethany with a small smile before looking at the crowd filling the stands.

It looked like most of Garland and a lot of tourists showed up for the charity fashion show tonight.

"Ladies and gentleman," I announced, my voice echoing throughout the ice rink. "Our guest of honor has arrived." I raised my hand towards Bethany, whose hands came to her mouth in surprise. "Please give a round of applause to the one and only Bethany Hart!"

The crowd began clapping so loud my ears rang, and I heard plenty of cheers from the section where the sewing club sat on the risers. I saw her parents and Eli slip into a reserved space along the rink walls, cheering with everyone else.

Bethany slipped out of her coat and made her way to me, walking slowly down the runway in her gorgeous green dress. I always thought she was pretty, but tonight? She took my breath away. Her hips swayed as she walked down the runway, and her tentative smile was right on me.

Somehow, I found the wherewithal to speak, reading from the card I prepared. "Bethany has had a passion for fashion design since she learned the impact of inclusive designs at eight years old. Ever since then, she's worked to help every woman, no matter what her size, feel beautiful in her skin by designing clothes for every shape and size. I've personally witnessed her work harder than anyone I've ever seen to make this fashion show happen and earn a spot at her dream fashion school this summer. I can't think of anyone else who deserves it more."

I glanced up from the card, seeing her face had turned a light shade of crimson at my words. As she looked around and took in the applause, I saw her lift her chin up and walk a little more proudly.

"Now, there were a few mishaps along the way that almost meant this fashion show didn't happen. But so many people in Garland came together to make this happen. We believe in you, Bethany, and we know that everyone deserves to see your gorgeous designs and hard work."

She met my eyes as she got closer and I grinned at her. She smiled back, and her green eyes sparkled like the ice all around her.

Just her smile was worth all the effort I'd put in the last three days to make this happen.

More than anything, I just wanted everything to come together for her application because she really did deserve a spot in the program.

Bethany stood next to me. "I can't believe you

did this," she said quietly, looking around at all the decorations. "How?"

"Let's just say... a little Garland magic," I told her, flicking off the microphone so the conversation could stay just between us. "The dry cleaner volunteered to clean all of the designs, and the sewing club worked around the clock to patch up everything that got torn."

I saw a tear run down her cheek. "I just can't believe it," she said. "Thank you, Kane. And I'm sorry for all the mean things I said."

I wiped away the tear and gave her a hug. "It's okay," I said. "I just couldn't bear to not see you have this moment."

She hugged me back, tight, and I didn't want the moment to end, but it was time to get the show started. And hopefully everything would come together as planned and it would be more than a fashion show—it would be the start of a movement. The start of her dreams coming true.

This was her time to shine.

25

BETHANY

usic began playing from the playlist I'd created for the original fashion show. The notes filled the entire ice rink and made my heart beat faster. The crowd began clapping.

Nothing like this had ever happened to me before. Part of me was sure I was dreaming, except for the feel of Kane's hand in mine. It made me realize that maybe I could have both—the boyfriend and my dreams. I didn't have to choose. Not when it came to Kane.

That's when I realized the music over the speakers wasn't the same. Well, it was, but it was just the instrumental music and a choir of voices was singing the words. I turned to see the Carol

Karens singing their hearts out. They wore something I'd never seen them in before–candy cane striped dresses and fur-lined hats. They looked like Santa's elves.

Then, Kane nudged me, and I realized a model was starting down the runway in my first design.

It was a short green dress with dramatic sleeves. I had the most fun ever envisioning and bringing to life. And there it was for everyone to see. I lifted the microphone to my mouth and heard my voice echo around the rink as I talked about my inspiration for the design–Mrs. Cole's Candy Making shop. I loved seeing the candy pull apart on the wheel in the window–that was the inspiration for the sleeves.

The model reached the end of the runway, and a camera flashed. I spotted the professional photographer capturing every moment. I turned to Kane, my jaw dropping. "You got a photographer?" I whispered.

He nodded. "I knew you'd want to remember this moment."

My heart warmed. But I didn't have time to bask in the feeling because the next model was starting down the runway.

"This pantsuit is perfect for an upscale holiday

party," I said. "Curvy women deserve to have professional, tailored outfits designed for their curves without needing to shove themselves into shapewear."

The crowd cheered, encouraging me to keep going.

"This design was inspired by the nutcracker men standing outside Santa's Bag," I said. My eyes started to fill with tears because the town had inspired these designs, and they'd also given me a platform to share them.

Up next, the model wearing the untouched white and green matching set started down the runway. I smiled, seeing it shaping perfectly for her body. "This outfit is perfect for someone who wants to travel stylishly and comfortably to see their family or maybe even tour the cutest Christmas town ever."

The cheering got even louder then.

"It has a drawstring waist to accommodate different body shapes and short sleeves so you can layer it to your comfort," I finished. The model reached the end of the runway and posed for photos.

I grinned, seeing her posing perfectly to show

off the design. I couldn't help thinking these photos would look so good with my application.

Up next was a poofy green dress with a tulle skirt and sharper bodice. "This dress is perfect for a winter dance and inspired by the leaves at Mistletoe Hill." My cheeks flushed thinking now that Kane and I were on good terms, maybe I'd get to kiss him at the rock there like all the other couples did. But I continued, "I added detachable sleeves for those who need more support and a ribbon corset back so it can accommodate different bust sizes."

More cheers rang out, and that's when I saw all my friends standing along the rink... with boys beside them. We'd have so much catching up to do at Haley's holiday party.

Then a model began walking in a red pair of flowy velvet trousers and a matching oversized tunic with a square neckline and slits down the side to fit different waist sizes comfortably. There was a golden tassel belt around the waist to accentuate her figure. "This outfit is inspired by Its a Wonderful Film," I said. "Everyone knows going to the theater and waiting for the red curtains to open is a must in Garland." I smiled at Kane thinking about watching "The Holiday" with him.

It was crazy to think we almost kissed that night. "Plus, it's nice and soft for lifting up the armrest and cuddling up with your date."

Kane cheered at that, making my cheeks warm.

As the models started down the catwalk in a line to show off all the designs, I turned to Kane, fresh tears in my eyes. "I can't believe this. This is better than I ever could've imagined myself."

He squeezed my hand. "You deserve this and more. Now, it's time to walk the runway one last time."

I didn't have time to second guess myself as he nudged me toward the carpet. I saw flashes. I heard a low roar that I quickly realized was people clapping with the sound of the music. Then I blinked and realized this was it.

This was my moment.

They were cheering for me.

I pushed my shoulders back, held my chin high, and walked like I'd never walked before.

The sound of people clapping and cheering grew even more, and I couldn't believe this was real life.

When I reached the end of the runway again, Kane was there, smiling from ear to ear.

Before I could think about it too much, I walked straight into his arms.

Then I kissed him, not caring who was watching.

I just wanted him to know how much he meant to me.

Not just because of everything he had done to make this fashion show come true, but every day since we'd met as kids.

I'd never let anything get in our way again.

Then the sound of someone coughing and clearing their throat nearby caught me off guard.

I pulled away from Kane, then turned around to find out who had joined us on stage.

BETHANY

*a*n older man stood behind us, several feet away.

It looked like he'd walked over from an opening in the railing not far away.

"Bethany Hart?" he asked. He held a yellow notepad and pen in his hands, and I saw several scribbles there before trying to figure out who he was. He didn't look familiar.

"Yes?" I said, taking a small step away from Kane, considering how close we'd just been.

He came close and extended his hand to me. I took it.

"Charles Brooks," he said. "I'm one of the admissions chairs for Future Fashion Icon."

My jaw felt open. I couldn't help it. I turned to

159

Kane, just to make sure I'd heard correctly, and he *winked* at me.

I turned back to Mr. Brooks, putting my jaw back into place. "Oh my goodness, I can't believe you're here."

All of a sudden, I kind of wished I hadn't just kissed Kane like that in front of practically all of Garland. And one of the admissions chairs!

Another part of me didn't regret a thing.

"Thank you for coming," I stammered.

He nodded, giving me a small smile. "It's not something we usually do, but my wife and I are visiting Garland, so I had to see for myself." He glanced around. "What you did here tonight was impressive."

"Thank you," I exhaled, glancing at Kane again, who still had a grin on his face. "It was really a community effort."

"But the designs. They're all yours?" Mr. Brooks asked.

I nodded vigorously. "Yes. I've been working on them for some time, actually."

He seemed impressed, but I also wondered if I was imagining things. This had to be a dream. Could I pinch myself without him noticing?

"Well, I look forward to seeing your application

and officially offering you a spot," he said. "But it's safe to say… we'll see you this summer."

I brought my hands to my mouth. When I finally got it together, I thanked him again.

"Congratulations on all of your hard work," he said, offering one last smile. "Now, I had the most exquisite cup of hot cocoa I've ever had in my life earlier, and I must have another before I head home. If you'll excuse me."

And with that and a tip of his fedora, he was gone.

I turned back to Kane. "Oh my gosh," I cried, happy tears falling down my cheeks in chilly rivers.

He hugged me, hard, and I hugged him back.

"Kane, I definitely didn't deserve this," I said. "You went above and beyond."

He pulled back and looked at me. "Yes, you do, and don't make me argue with you right now," he said with a chuckle.

Then he kissed me as if to ensure my silence.

The DJ kept the music going and we finally pulled apart.

With my family and friends approaching, I had to part from Kane. At least for now. I thanked everyone I saw for coming, especially Eli for sneakily making sure I wore this dress. I couldn't thank the sewing club ladies enough. I couldn't believe all the work they'd put in not once but twice for me.

I gave my grandmother a big hug, and then my parents enveloped me in a group hug.

My friends all told me how much they enjoyed the show and promised to give me all the details of their new loves at the holiday party.

After we cleaned up Fall La La La, leaving the ice rink like we'd found it, everyone made their way across the street to Scrooge's.

It was time to celebrate.

KANE

Bethany, her family, the sewing club, and several others kept the party going at Scrooge's.

Which, of course, Scrooge *loved*. If Scrooge hated anything in the world as much as Christmas, it was a loud, fun, full-of-laughter party.

But he put up with us and said dinner was on the house. I swore I saw him smile when he thought no one was looking. Bethany gave him a big hug, which he promptly complained about.

That made Bethany's grandma laugh. "He really is a big teddy bear down inside, you know," she confided to me.

"Deep, deep inside," I added dryly.

"I remember him growing up," she whispered. "You wouldn't believe what a sweet kid he was."

I analyzed Scrooge from afar. "Really?"

"Really," she said. Then she went off to sit with the sewing club ladies, conveniently leaving me with Bethany at our booth in the corner.

I reached my hand across the table to hold Bethany's and gave it a squeeze.

I couldn't believe how well the fashion show had worked out. Everything had been perfect, and now I was sitting here with the most beautiful girl in the world.

Bethany met my gaze and smiled. "Thank you," she said. I noticed tears in her eyes. Hopefully more happy tears.

I gave her hand another squeeze. "I hope you know I don't want to be a distraction for you. I want us both to lift each other up."

She shook her head. "I'm sorry I said that, Kane. I was so wrong. I still can't believe you invited the chair. I mean, how did you even find his contact information? Much less get him to come down here?"

I shrugged. "Let's just say I'm quite persistent when I want to be."

She grinned. But then her smile fell. "Listen,

Kane" she said, staring at her hand in mine. "I still need to apologize… for everything I said."

I immediately got up and went over to her side of the booth so we could sit close. She moved over and made room for me.

I put my arm around her, glad I could finally do that after wishing for years that I could. "It's okay," I said. "I understand why you were so upset."

She shook her head. "It's no excuse for how I talked to you that day, Kane, and I'm sorry. I really am."

I kissed her forehead, soaking in how good it felt to hear those words. But now all I wanted to do was move past it.

I wanted a future with Bethany, that didn't leave a lot of time to worry about the past.

BETHANY WAS OFFICIALLY my girlfriend as we walked hand in hand to the New Year's Eve party through the recently cleared sidewalk. At least six inches of snow had fallen the night before and there were big mounds of the stuff lining the sidewalks and roads.

Up ahead, I saw the Garland Christmas tree

sparkling, its bright lights illuminating the square. In just a couple days, it would come down and we wouldn't see it again for almost a year.

I couldn't believe it. Just seeing it reminded me of all the amazing things that had happened over the holidays. So much could change in such little time.

Just over a week ago, I'd wished upon its star to finally have a chance with Bethany thinking that it would never happen.

And here we were, an official couple.

Bethany gave me a small nudge. "You're being quiet. What's on your mind?"

I smiled and nodded towards the Christmas tree. "I was thinking of the wish I made. I just realized it came true."

"Really?" she said.

I squeezed her hand and smiled. She smiled back.

She stopped walking and so did I. She turned to me. "Actually, I wished for something that day too."

"What was it?" I asked.

"To earn a spot in the fashion program," she said quietly. "And even with everything that happened, my wish still came true." A second later, she went on. "What about you? What did you wish for?"

I brought my forehead down until it gently touched hers. "I wished for a chance to finally be with you," I told her.

All around us, snowflakes slowly made their way down from the sky. I saw a couple land on Bethany's long eyelashes.

I pulled Bethany close to me, until both our eyes closed and my mouth found hers.

It looked like Garland magic was real after all.

RETURN TO GARLAND with more holiday romance stories in the Curvy Girl Christmas series!

AUTHOR'S NOTE

I have a confession to make: I am not a fashionista. I'm not great at pairing outfits together and most of the time I'm wearing an over-sized t-shirt and a pair of leggings. (Biker shorts if it's too hot outside.) But I love watching fashion shows.

Growing up, I was obsessed with shows like Project Runway and America's Next Top Model. Seeing people's creativity and pretending like I was a judge was so much fun. Every now and then, I still quote Tim Gunn when I'm in a pinch. *"Designers, make it work."* I even got to see Austin Scarlett, a former Project Runway designer, at a fashion show at Kansas State University and felt like I was living my best life as I got his autograph.

So I'm *thrilled* I got to write a fashion show into

one of these books. If it ever gets turned into a movie or a television show, that's the scene I'm most looking forward to! Describing the outfits for that scene was definitely challenging, but I hope you enjoyed it!

Even though I'll never be a fashion designer or a runway model, it's fun to embrace all areas of creativity. Never feel like you have to be perfect at something to enjoy it! If you want to write, write for the fun of it. If you like painting, whip out that brush and a watercolor set. Enjoy it without the pressure of being perfect, because creativity makes life so much fun!

ACKNOWLEDGMENTS

I'm so excited this body positive Christmas story is out in the world! I have a few people to thank, so let me make it short and sweet like this story!

My husband and children – you rock (around the Christmas tree! ;))

Team Kelsie – thank you for taking such good care of my readers and me!

Yesenia Vargas – thank you for your help with this story! I couldn't have done it without you!

Jordan Truex – thank you for your expert editing skills! Short novels aren't always easy for me to write, so thank you for making this one better!

Courtney Encheff and Patrick Jean-Jacques – thank you for narrating this story and bringing it to life for my listeners!

Najla at Qamber Designs – thank you for the *gorgeous* cover design!

And you, Sweet reader – you make this

Christmas season even merrier. Thank you for reading!

ABOUT THE AUTHOR

Kelsie Stelting is a body positive romance author who writes love stories with strong characters, deep feelings, and happy endings.

You can often find her writing, spending time with family, and soaking up too much sun wherever she can find it.

Hang out with Kelsie in her online readers' group!

ALSO BY KELSIE STELTING

A Curvy Girl Christmas

Santa Loves Curvy Girls

A Curvy Carol

A Curvy Wonderland

Curvy All the Way

Curvy and Bright

The Curvy Girl Club

Curvy Girls Can't Date Quarterbacks

Curvy Girls Can't Date Billionaires

Curvy Girls Can't Date Cowboys

Curvy Girls Can't Date Bad Boys

Curvy Girls Can't Date Best Friends

Curvy Girls Can't Date Bullies

Curvy Girls Can't Dance

Curvy Girls Can't Date Soldiers

Curvy Girls Can't Date Princes

Curvy Girls Can't Date Rock Stars

Curvy Girls Can't Date Surfers

Curvy Girls Can't Date Point Guards

Curvy Girls Can't Date Curvy Girls (Pride Edition)

The Texas High Series

Abi and the Boy Next Door

Abi and the Boy Who Lied

Abi and the Boy She Loves

Chasing Skye

Becoming Skye

Loving Skye

Always Anika

The Pen Pal Romance Series

Dear Adam

Fabio Vs. the Friend Zone

Sincerely Cinderella

Standalone YA Romance

Road Trip with the Enemy

YA Contemporary Romance Anthologies

The Art of Taking Chances

Two More Days

Nonfiction

Raising the West

Printed in Dunstable, United Kingdom

Printed in Dunstable, United Kingdom